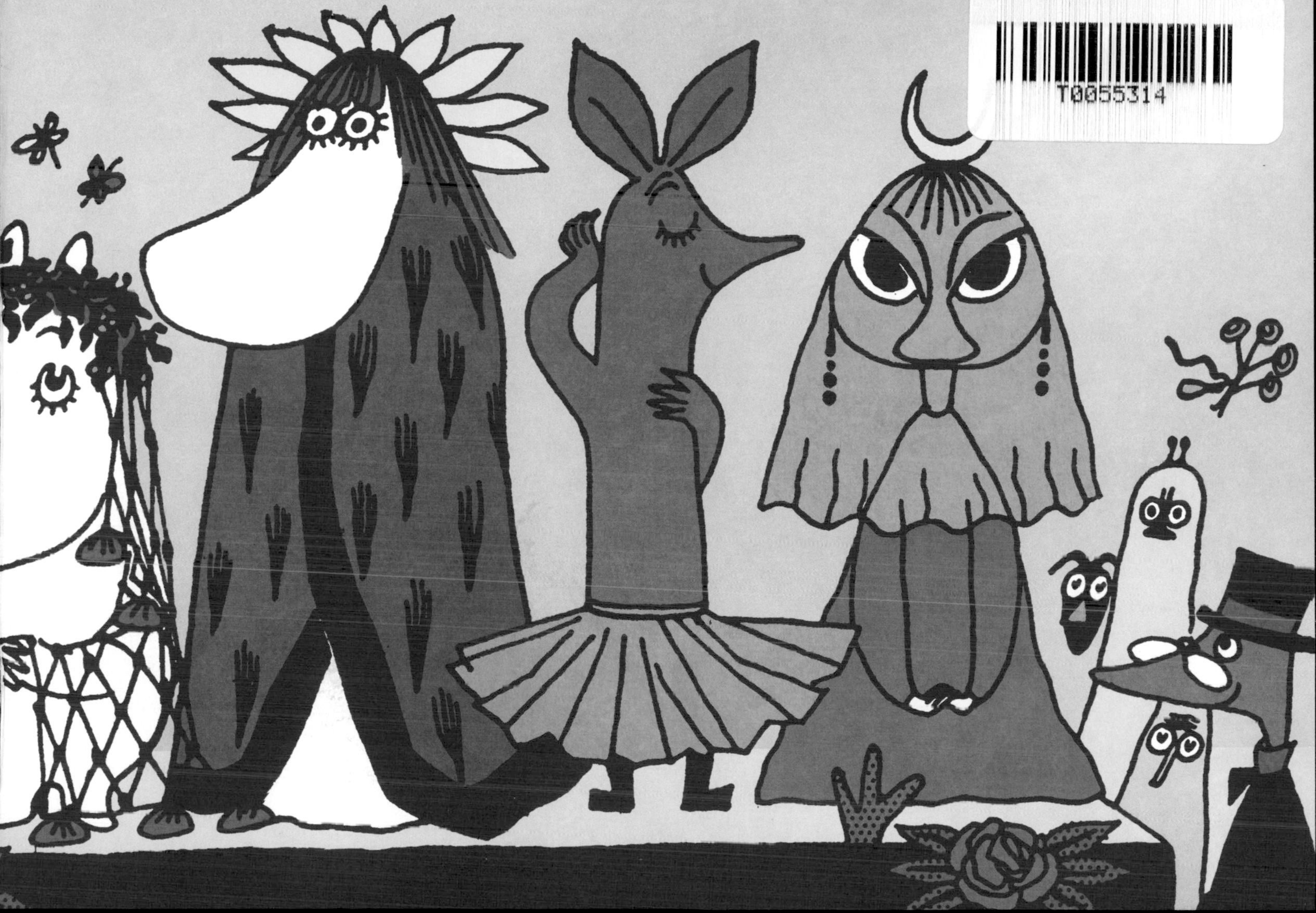

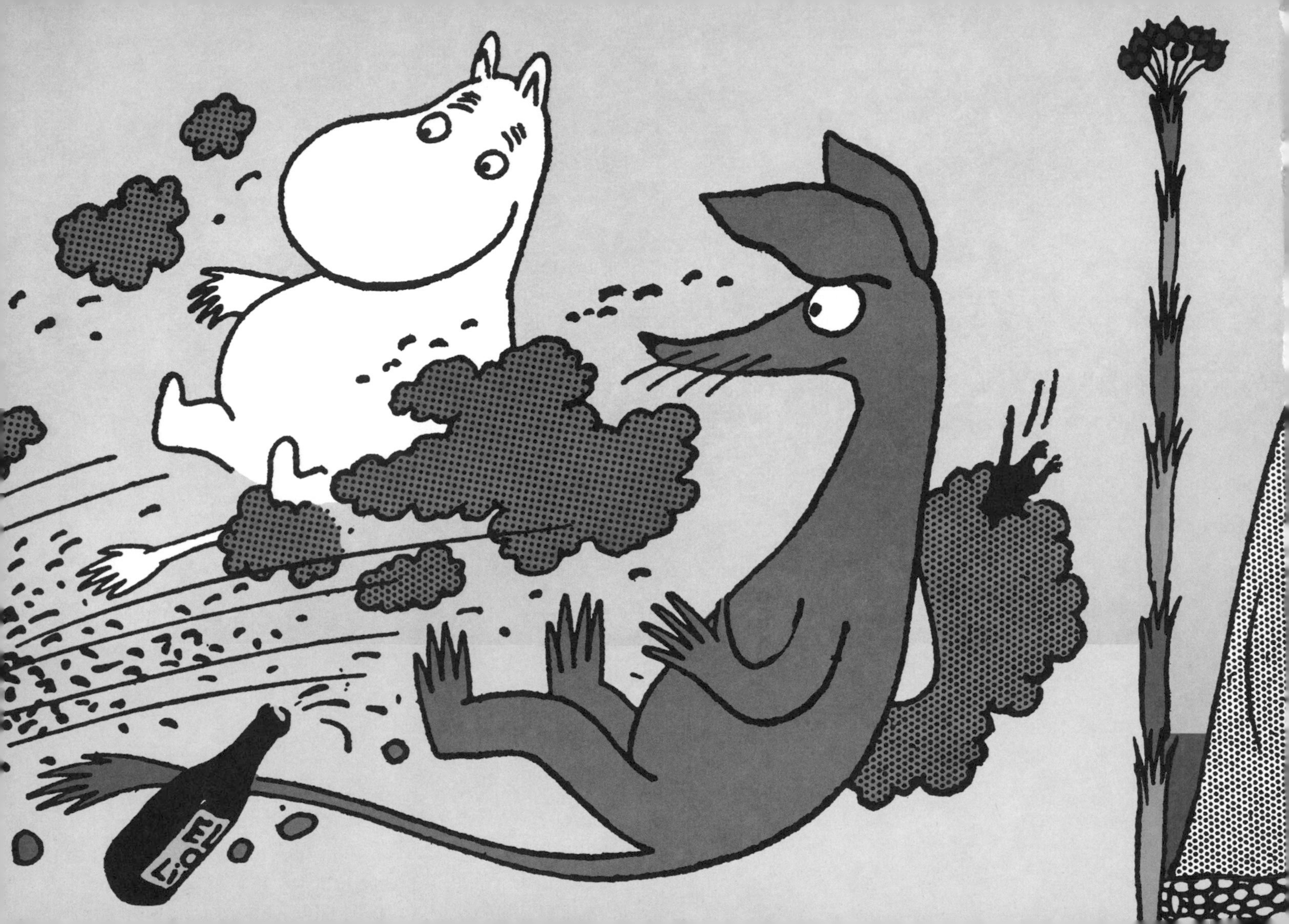

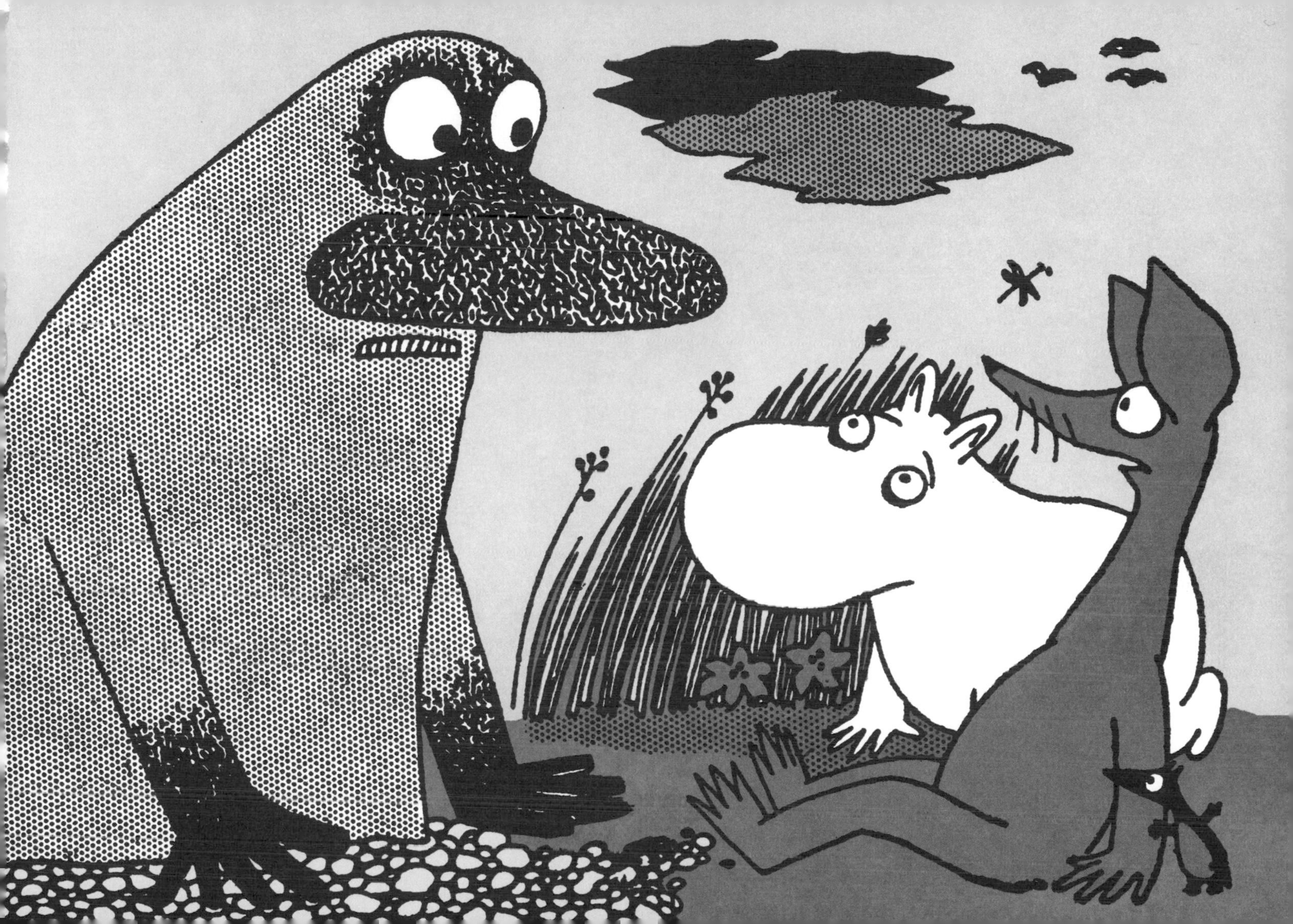

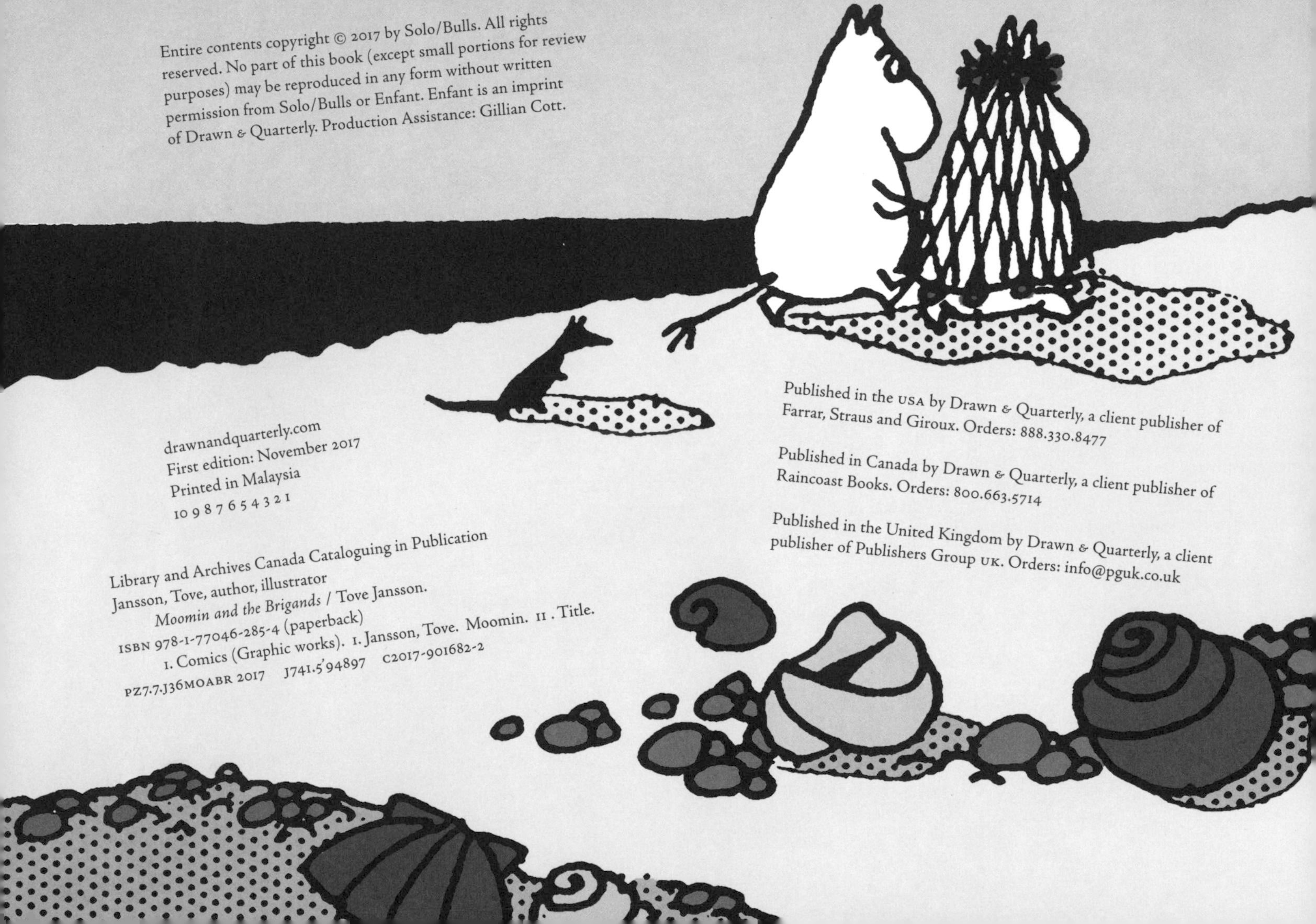

 Enfant is an imprint of Drawn & Quarterly. Production Assistance: Gillian Cott.

drawnandquarterly.com
First edition: November 2017
Printed in Malaysia
10 9 8 7 6 5 4 3 2 1

Library and Archives Canada Cataloguing in Publication
Jansson, Tove, author, illustrator
Moomin and the Brigands / Tove Jansson.
ISBN 978-1-77046-285-4 (paperback)
1. Comics (Graphic works). I. Jansson, Tove. Moomin. II. Title.
PZ7.7.J36MOABR 2017 J741.5'94897 C2017-901682-2

Published in the USA by Drawn & Quarterly, a client publisher of Farrar, Straus and Giroux. Orders: 888.330.8477

Published in Canada by Drawn & Quarterly, a client publisher of Raincoast Books. Orders: 800.663.5714

Published in the United Kingdom by Drawn & Quarterly, a client publisher of Publishers Group UK. Orders: info@pguk.co.uk

Tove Jansson

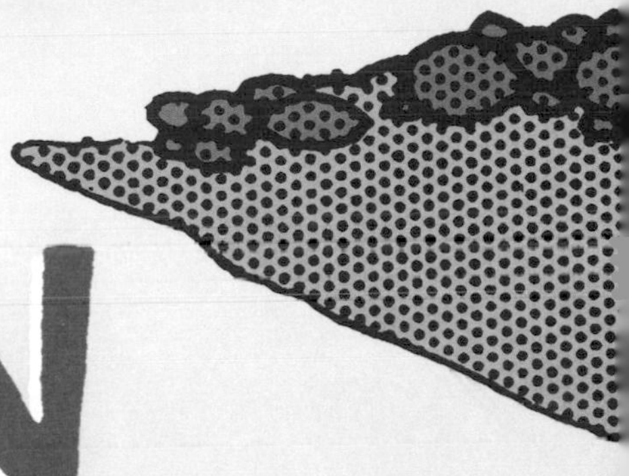

MOOMIN AND THE BRIGANDS

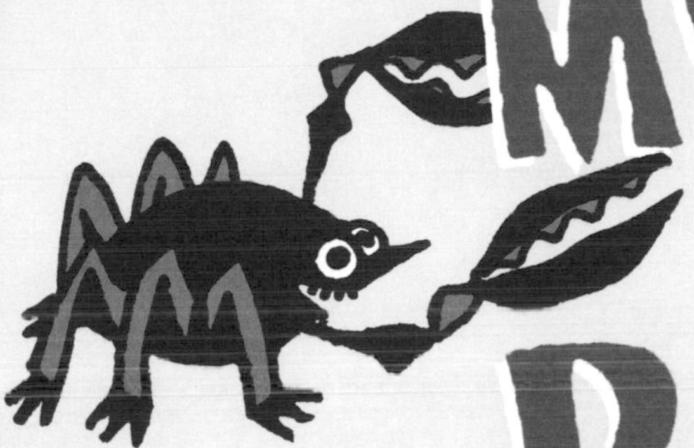

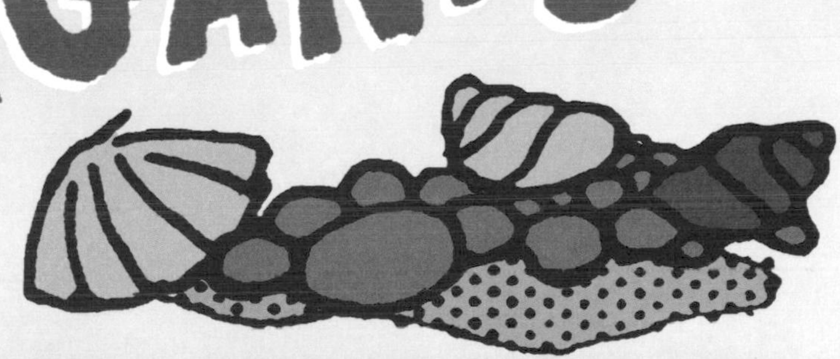

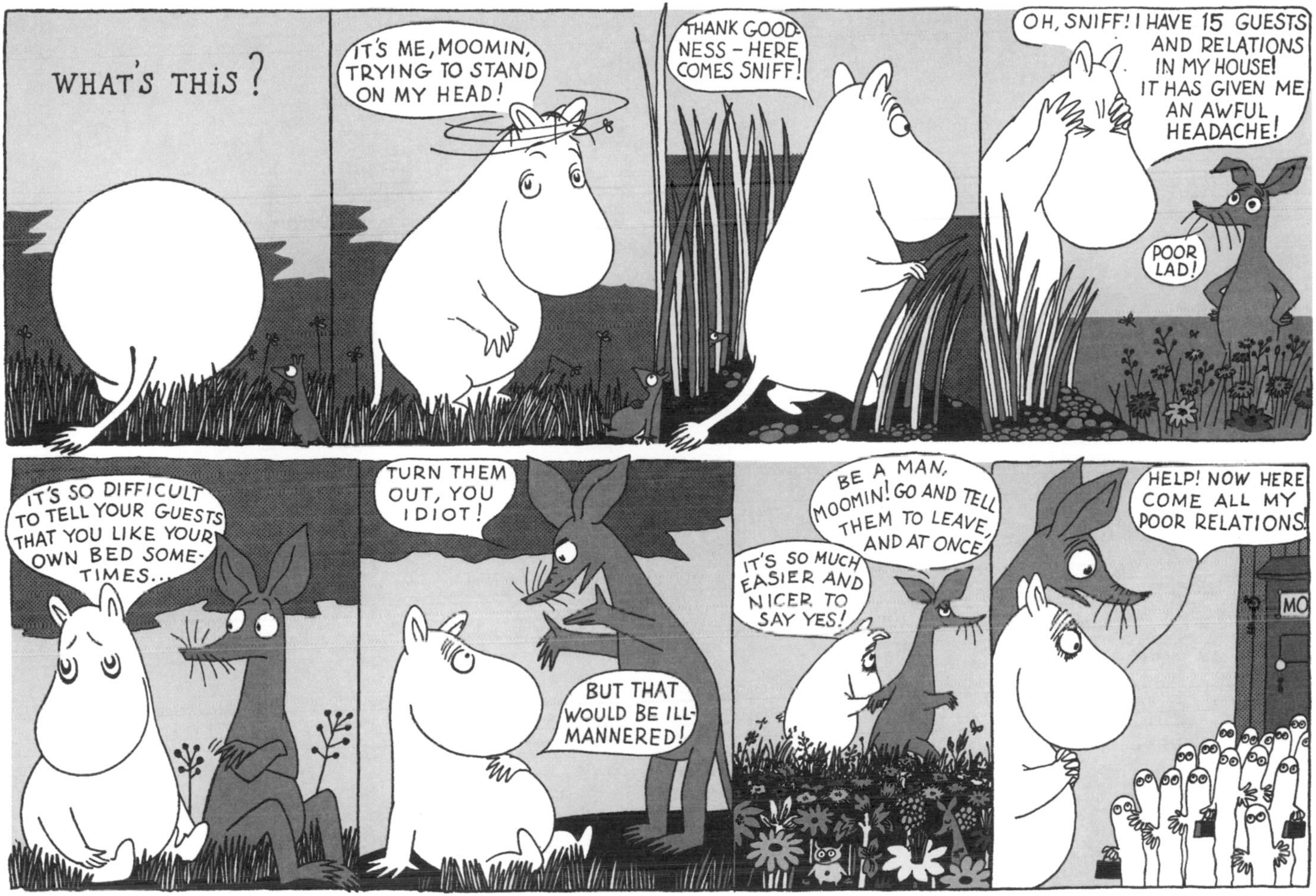
WHAT'S THIS?
IT'S ME, MOOMIN, TRYING TO STAND ON MY HEAD!
THANK GOODNESS – HERE COMES SNIFF!
OH, SNIFF! I HAVE 15 GUESTS AND RELATIONS IN MY HOUSE! IT HAS GIVEN ME AN AWFUL HEADACHE!
POOR LAD!
IT'S SO DIFFICULT TO TELL YOUR GUESTS THAT YOU LIKE YOUR OWN BED SOMETIMES...
TURN THEM OUT, YOU IDIOT!
BUT THAT WOULD BE ILL-MANNERED!
BE A MAN, MOOMIN! GO AND TELL THEM TO LEAVE, AND AT ONCE!
IT'S SO MUCH EASIER AND NICER TO SAY YES!
HELP! NOW HERE COME ALL MY POOR RELATIONS!
MO

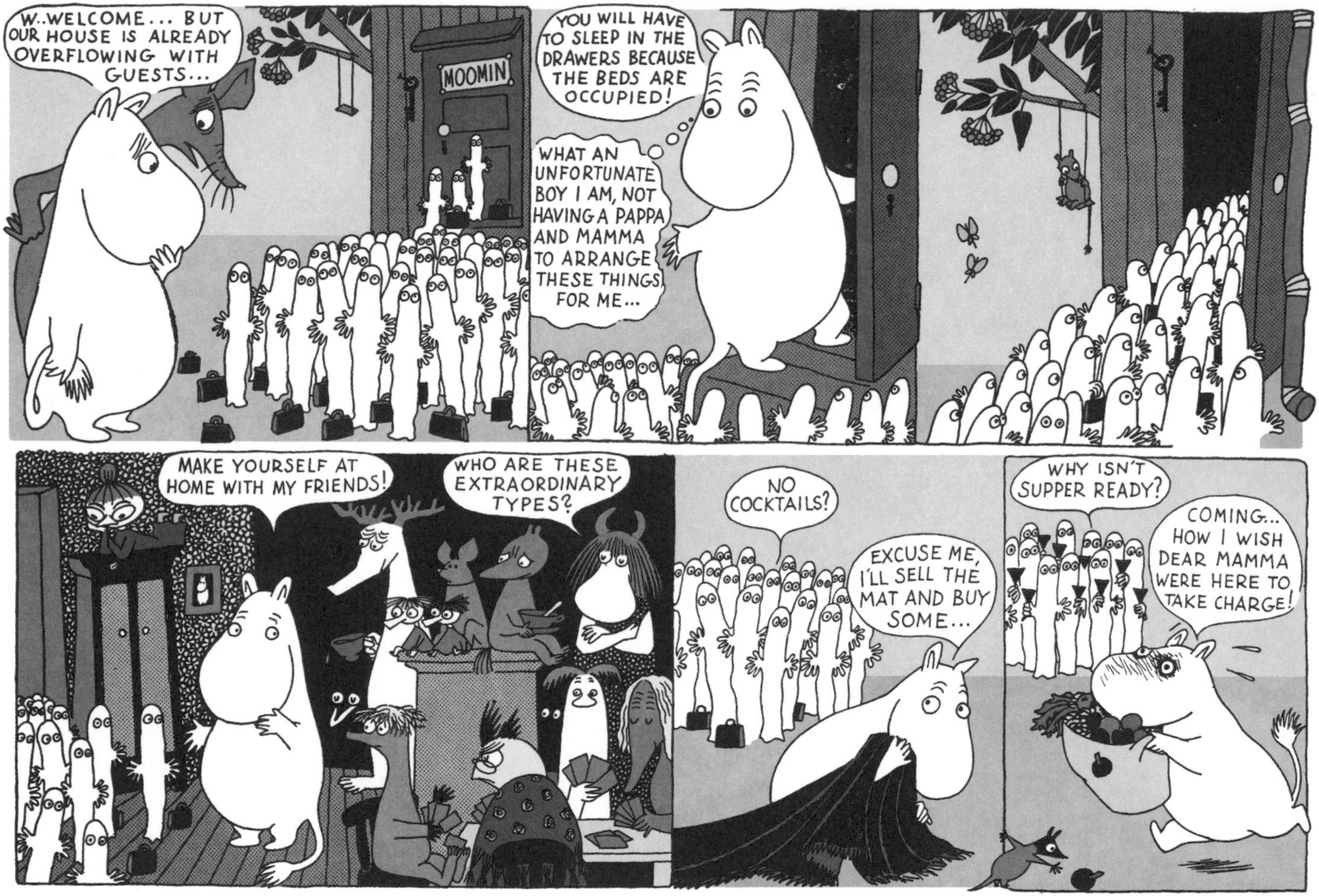
W..WELCOME... BUT OUR HOUSE IS ALREADY OVERFLOWING WITH GUESTS...
MOOMIN
YOU WILL HAVE TO SLEEP IN THE DRAWERS BECAUSE THE BEDS ARE OCCUPIED!
WHAT AN UNFORTUNATE BOY I AM, NOT HAVING A PAPPA AND MAMMA TO ARRANGE THESE THINGS FOR ME...
MAKE YOURSELF AT HOME WITH MY FRIENDS!
WHO ARE THESE EXTRAORDINARY TYPES?
NO COCKTAILS?
EXCUSE ME, I'LL SELL THE MAT AND BUY SOME...
WHY ISN'T SUPPER READY?
COMING... HOW I WISH DEAR MAMMA WERE HERE TO TAKE CHARGE!

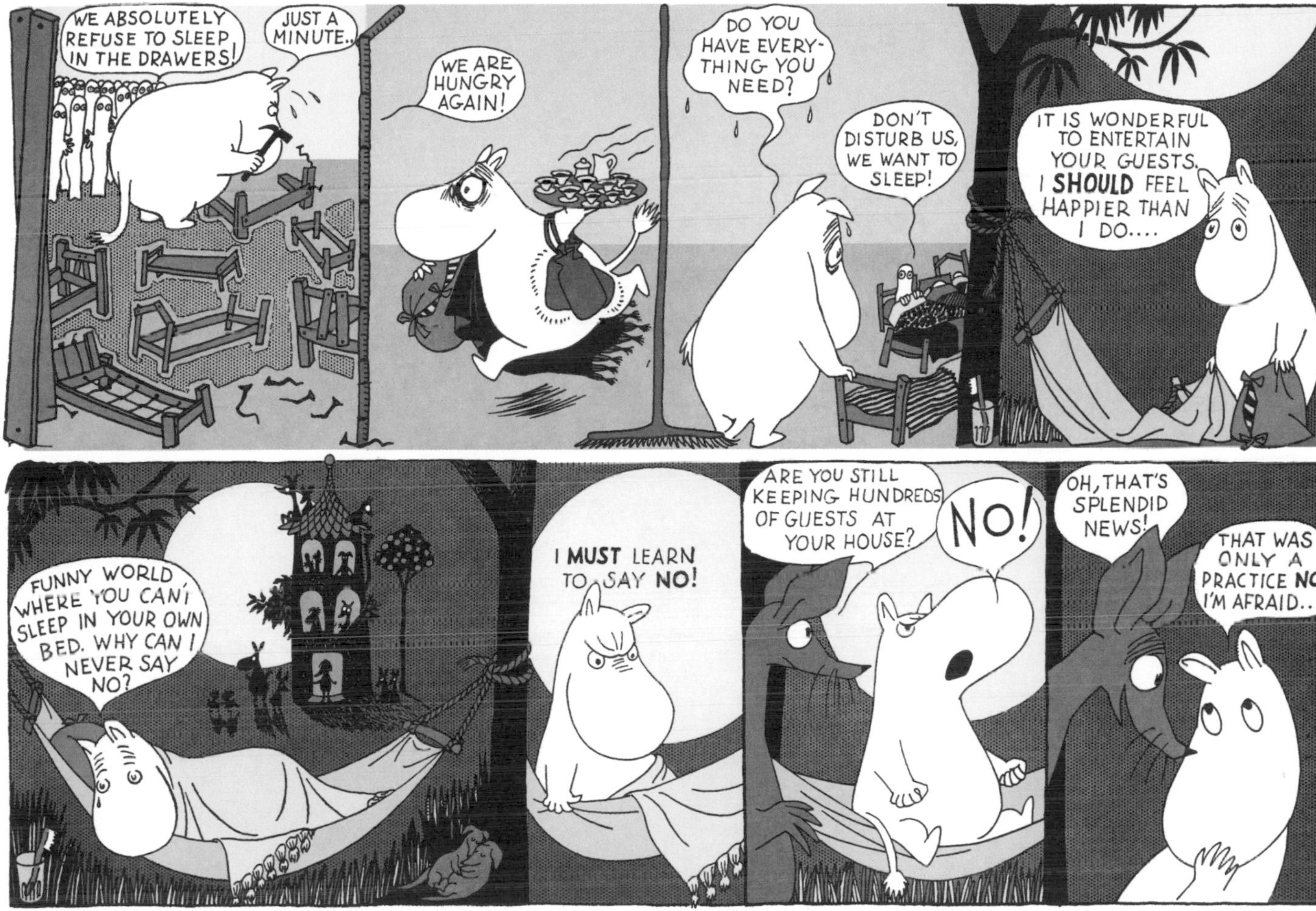

WE ABSOLUTELY REFUSE TO SLEEP IN THE DRAWERS!
JUST A MINUTE..
WE ARE HUNGRY AGAIN!
DO YOU HAVE EVERY-THING YOU NEED?
DON'T DISTURB US, WE WANT TO SLEEP!
IT IS WONDERFUL TO ENTERTAIN YOUR GUESTS. I **SHOULD** FEEL HAPPIER THAN I DO....
FUNNY WORLD WHERE YOU CAN'T SLEEP IN YOUR OWN BED. WHY CAN I NEVER SAY NO?
I **MUST** LEARN TO SAY **NO**!
ARE YOU STILL KEEPING HUNDREDS OF GUESTS AT YOUR HOUSE?
NO!
OH, THAT'S SPLENDID NEWS!
THAT WAS ONLY A PRACTICE **NO**, I'M AFRAID...

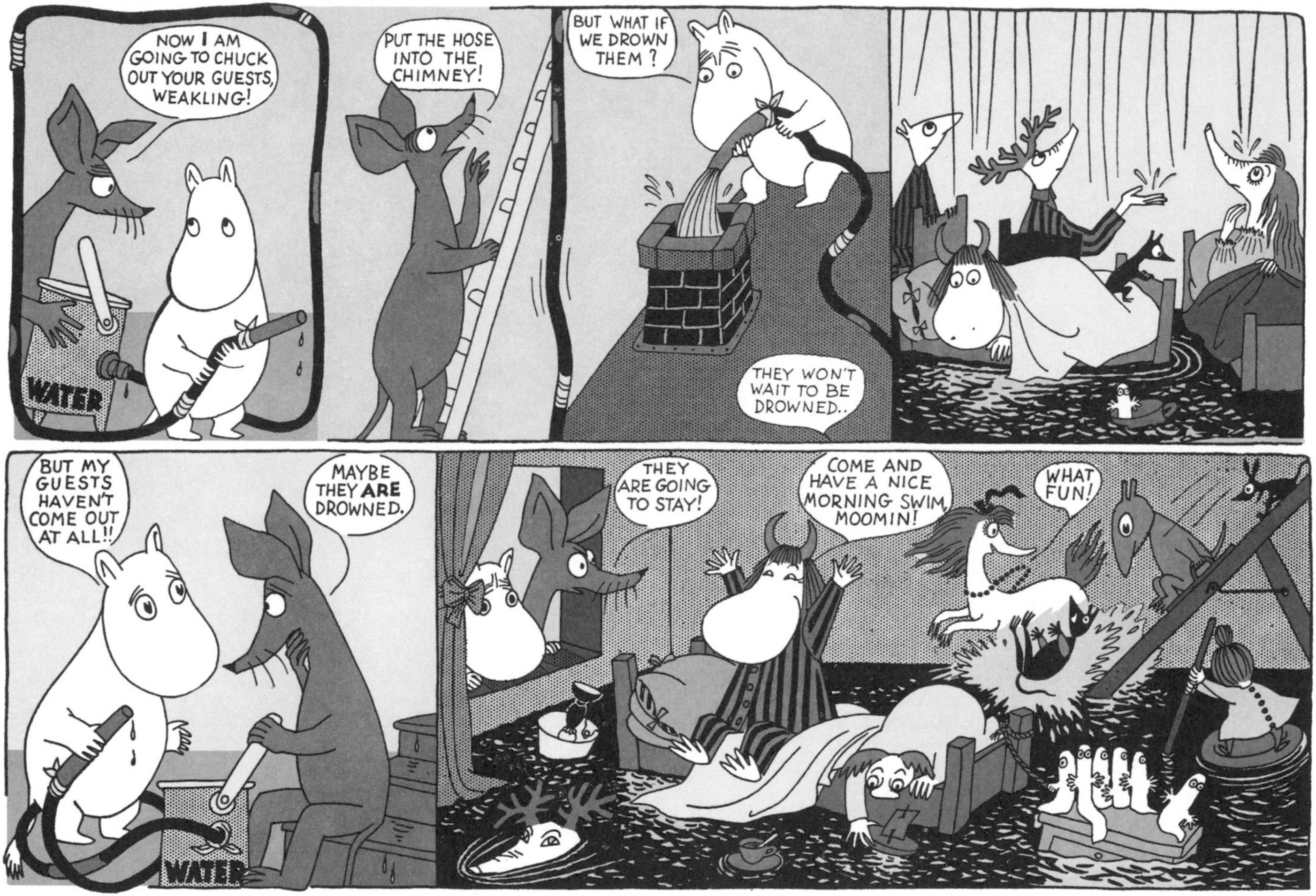
NOW I AM GOING TO CHUCK OUT YOUR GUESTS, WEAKLING!
WATER
PUT THE HOSE INTO THE CHIMNEY!
BUT WHAT IF WE DROWN THEM?
THEY WON'T WAIT TO BE DROWNED..
BUT MY GUESTS HAVEN'T COME OUT AT ALL!!
MAYBE THEY **ARE** DROWNED.
WATER
THEY ARE GOING TO STAY!
COME AND HAVE A NICE MORNING SWIM, MOOMIN!
WHAT FUN!

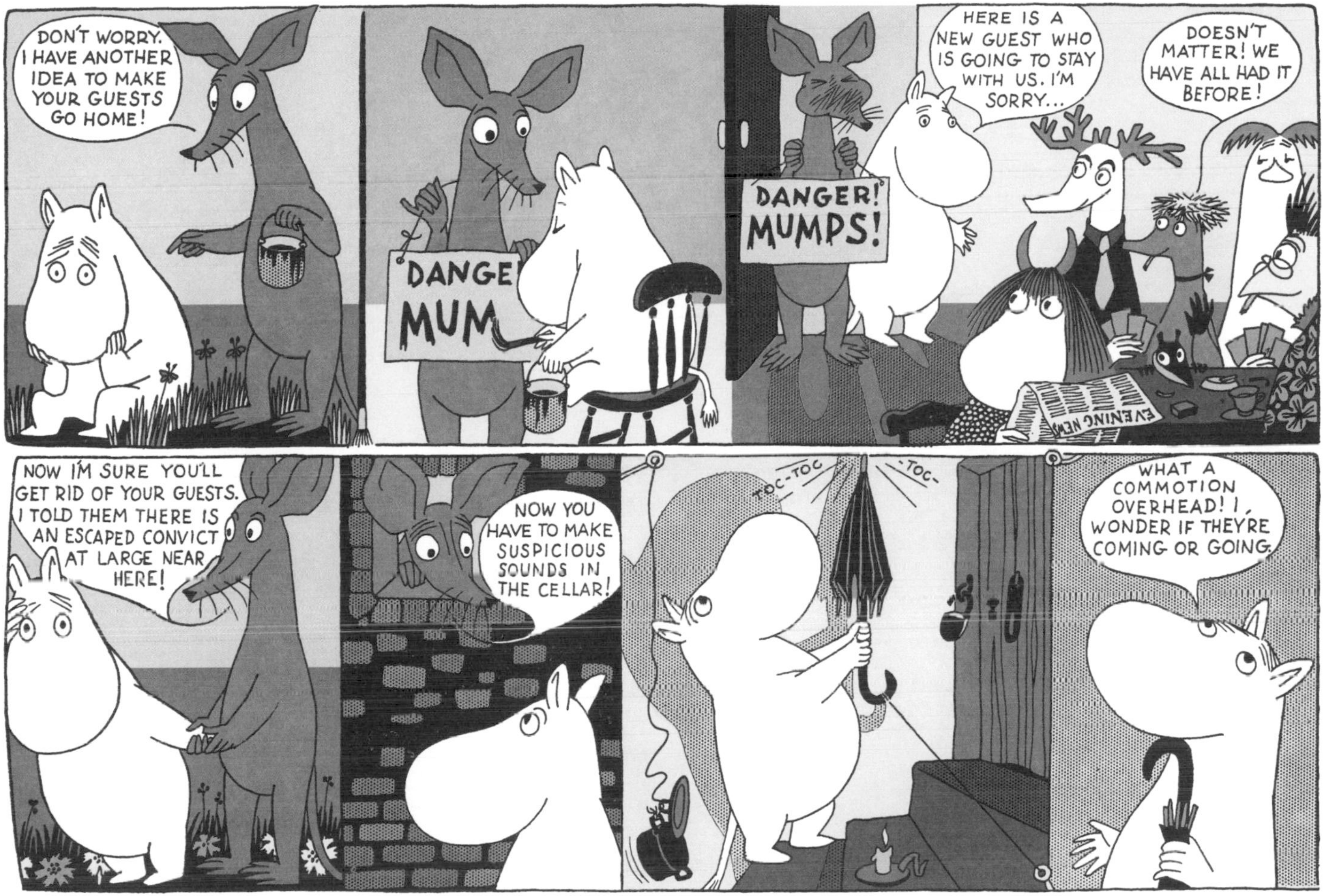
DON'T WORRY. I HAVE ANOTHER IDEA TO MAKE YOUR GUESTS GO HOME!
DANGE MUM
DANGER! MUMPS!
HERE IS A NEW GUEST WHO IS GOING TO STAY WITH US. I'M SORRY...
DOESN'T MATTER! WE HAVE ALL HAD IT BEFORE!
EVENING NEWS
NOW I'M SURE YOU'LL GET RID OF YOUR GUESTS. I TOLD THEM THERE IS AN ESCAPED CONVICT AT LARGE NEAR HERE!
NOW YOU HAVE TO MAKE SUSPICIOUS SOUNDS IN THE CELLAR!
TOC-TOC
-TOC-
WHAT A COMMOTION OVERHEAD! I WONDER IF THEY'RE COMING OR GOING.

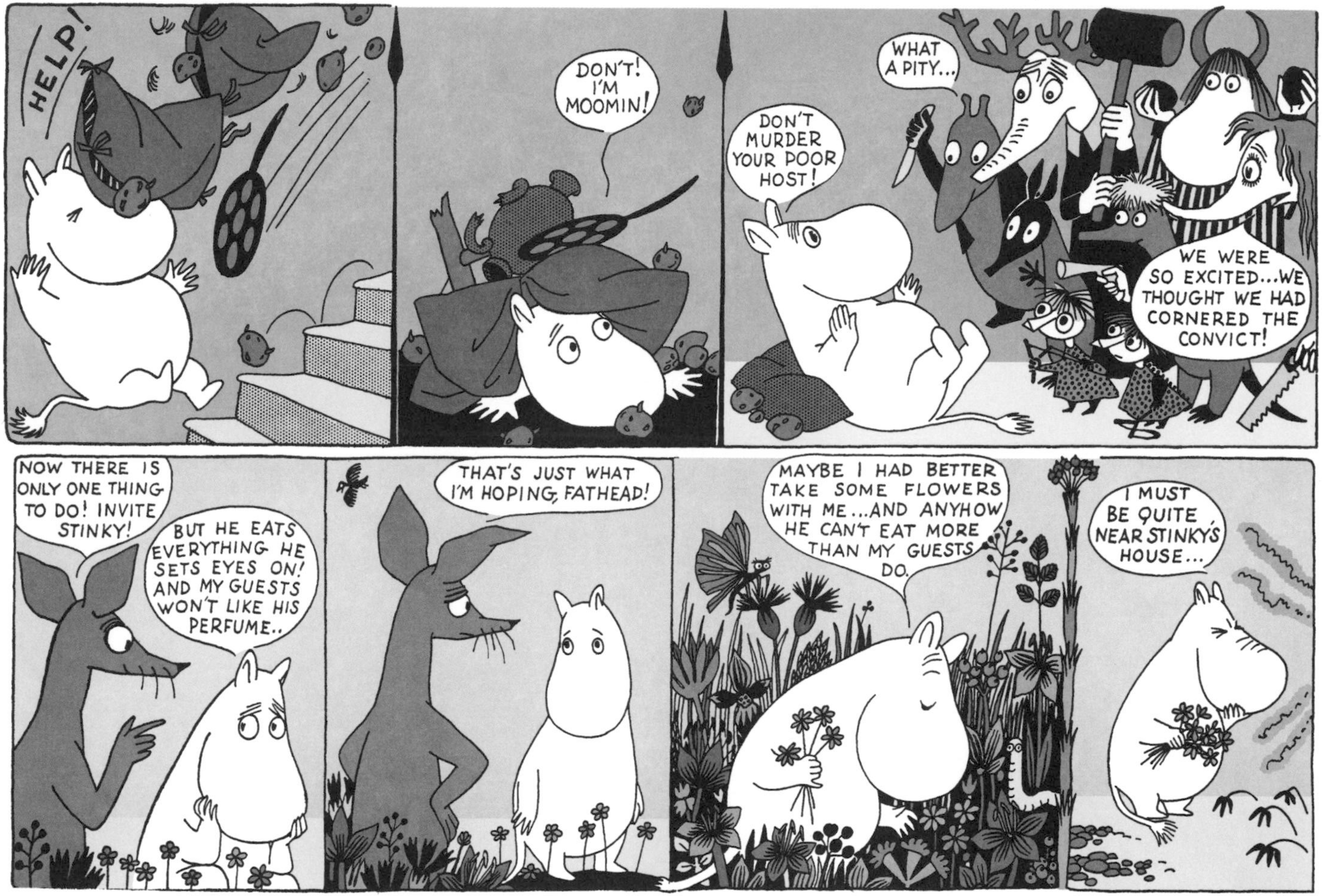
HELP!
DON'T! I'M MOOMIN!
DON'T MURDER YOUR POOR HOST!
WHAT A PITY...
WE WERE SO EXCITED...WE THOUGHT WE HAD CORNERED THE CONVICT!
NOW THERE IS ONLY ONE THING TO DO! INVITE STINKY!
BUT HE EATS EVERYTHING HE SETS EYES ON! AND MY GUESTS WON'T LIKE HIS PERFUME..
THAT'S JUST WHAT I'M HOPING, FATHEAD!
MAYBE I HAD BETTER TAKE SOME FLOWERS WITH ME...AND ANYHOW HE CAN'T EAT MORE THAN MY GUESTS DO.
I MUST BE QUITE NEAR STINKY'S HOUSE...

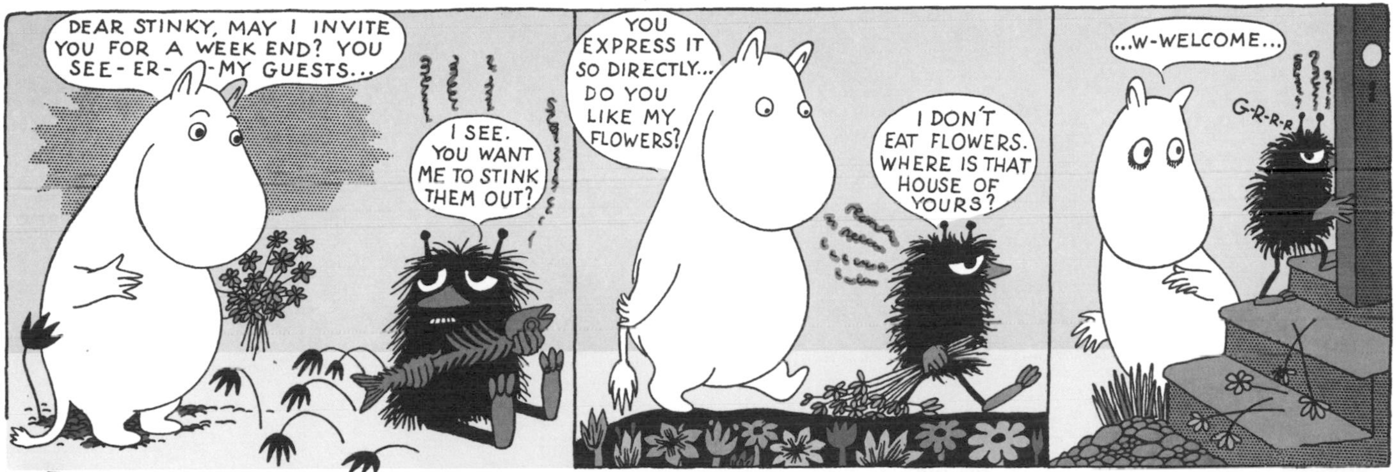
DEAR STINKY, MAY I INVITE YOU FOR A WEEK END? YOU SEE - ER- -MY GUESTS...
I SEE. YOU WANT ME TO STINK THEM OUT?
YOU EXPRESS IT SO DIRECTLY... DO YOU LIKE MY FLOWERS?
I DON'T EAT FLOWERS. WHERE IS THAT HOUSE OF YOURS?
...W-WELCOME...
G-R-R-R

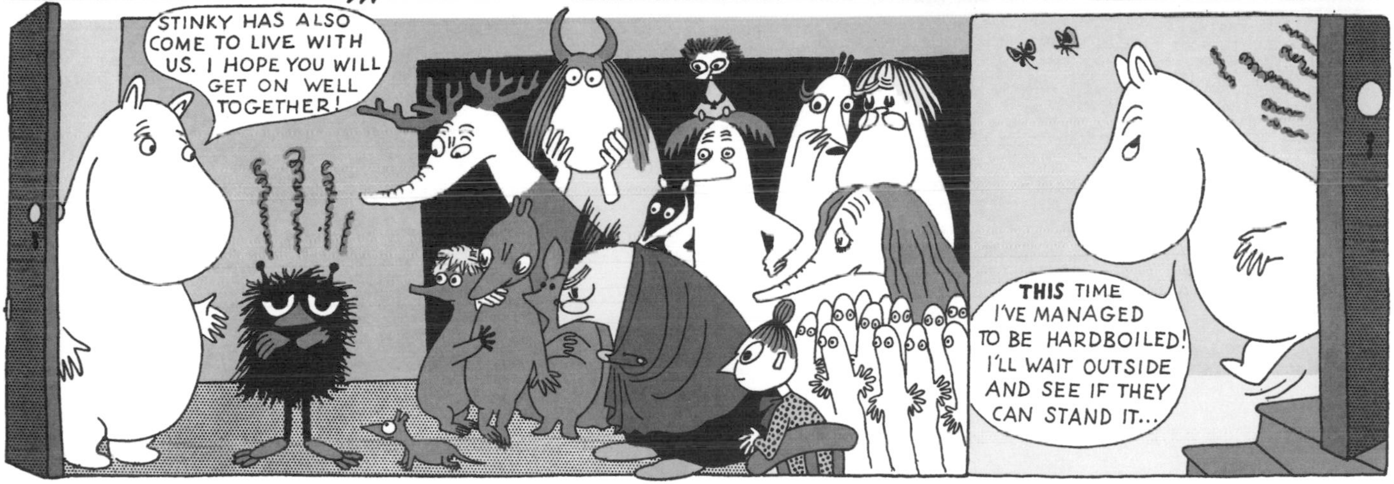
STINKY HAS ALSO COME TO LIVE WITH US. I HOPE YOU WILL GET ON WELL TOGETHER!
THIS TIME I'VE MANAGED TO BE HARDBOILED! I'LL WAIT OUTSIDE AND SEE IF THEY CAN STAND IT...

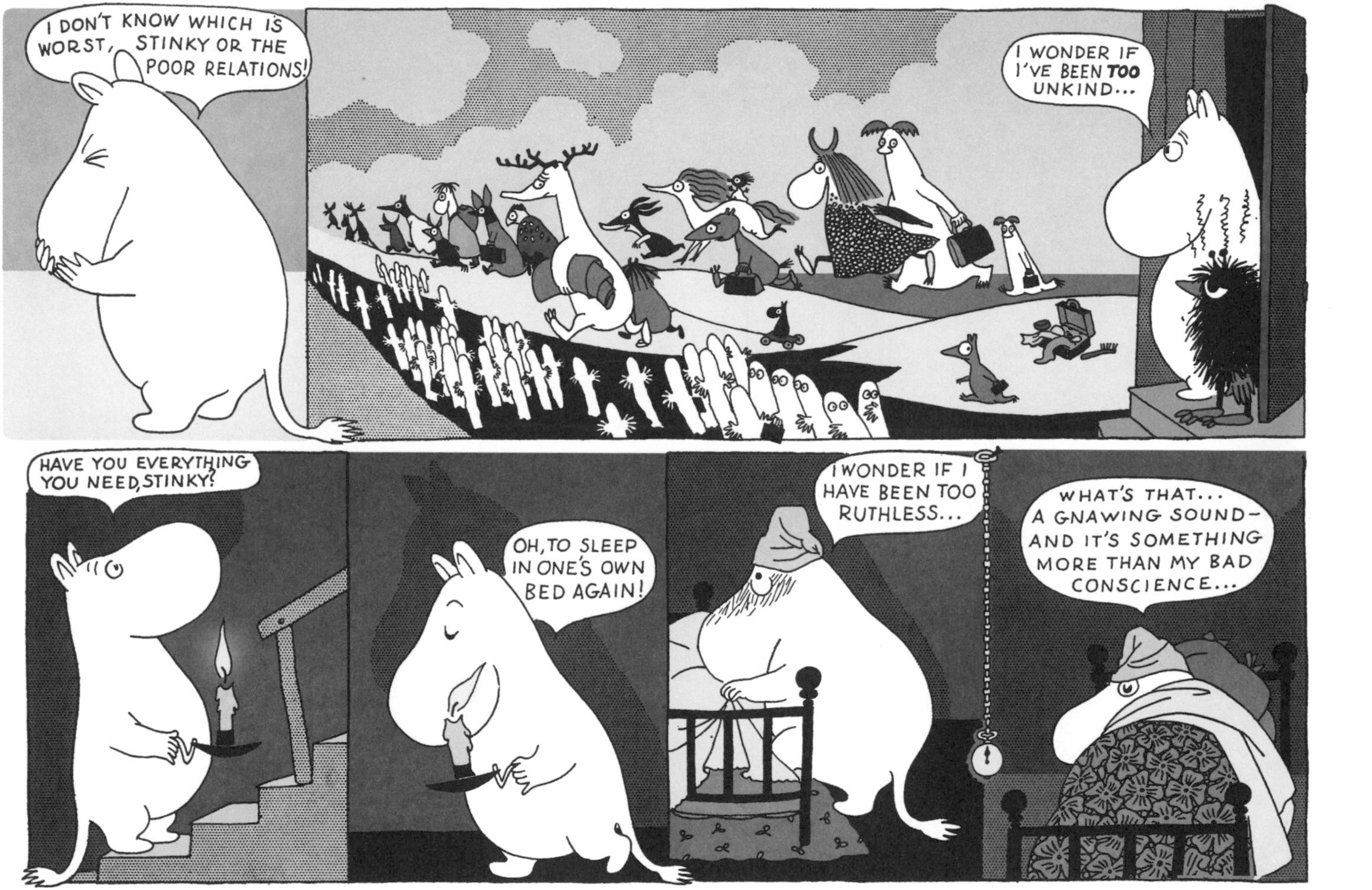
I DON'T KNOW WHICH IS WORST, STINKY OR THE POOR RELATIONS!
I WONDER IF I'VE BEEN **TOO** UNKIND...
HAVE YOU EVERYTHING YOU NEED, STINKY?
OH, TO SLEEP IN ONE'S OWN BED AGAIN!
I WONDER IF I HAVE BEEN TOO RUTHLESS...
WHAT'S THAT... A GNAWING SOUND— AND IT'S SOMETHING MORE THAN MY BAD CONSCIENCE...

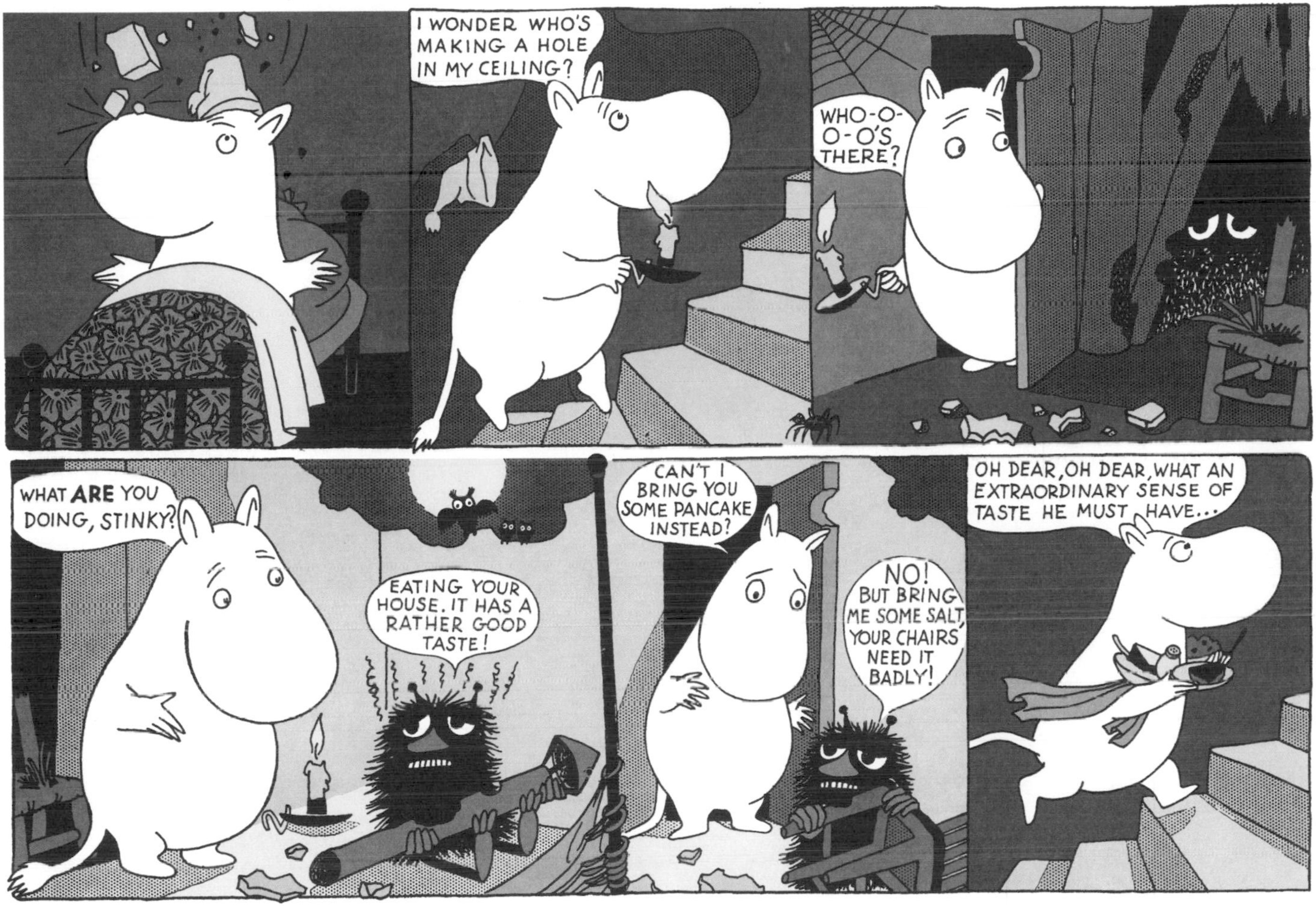
I WONDER WHO'S MAKING A HOLE IN MY CEILING?
WHO-O-O-O'S THERE?
WHAT **ARE** YOU DOING, STINKY?
EATING YOUR HOUSE. IT HAS A RATHER GOOD TASTE!
CAN'T I BRING YOU SOME PANCAKE INSTEAD?
NO! BUT BRING ME SOME SALT. YOUR CHAIRS NEED IT BADLY!
OH DEAR, OH DEAR, WHAT AN EXTRAORDINARY SENSE OF TASTE HE MUST HAVE...

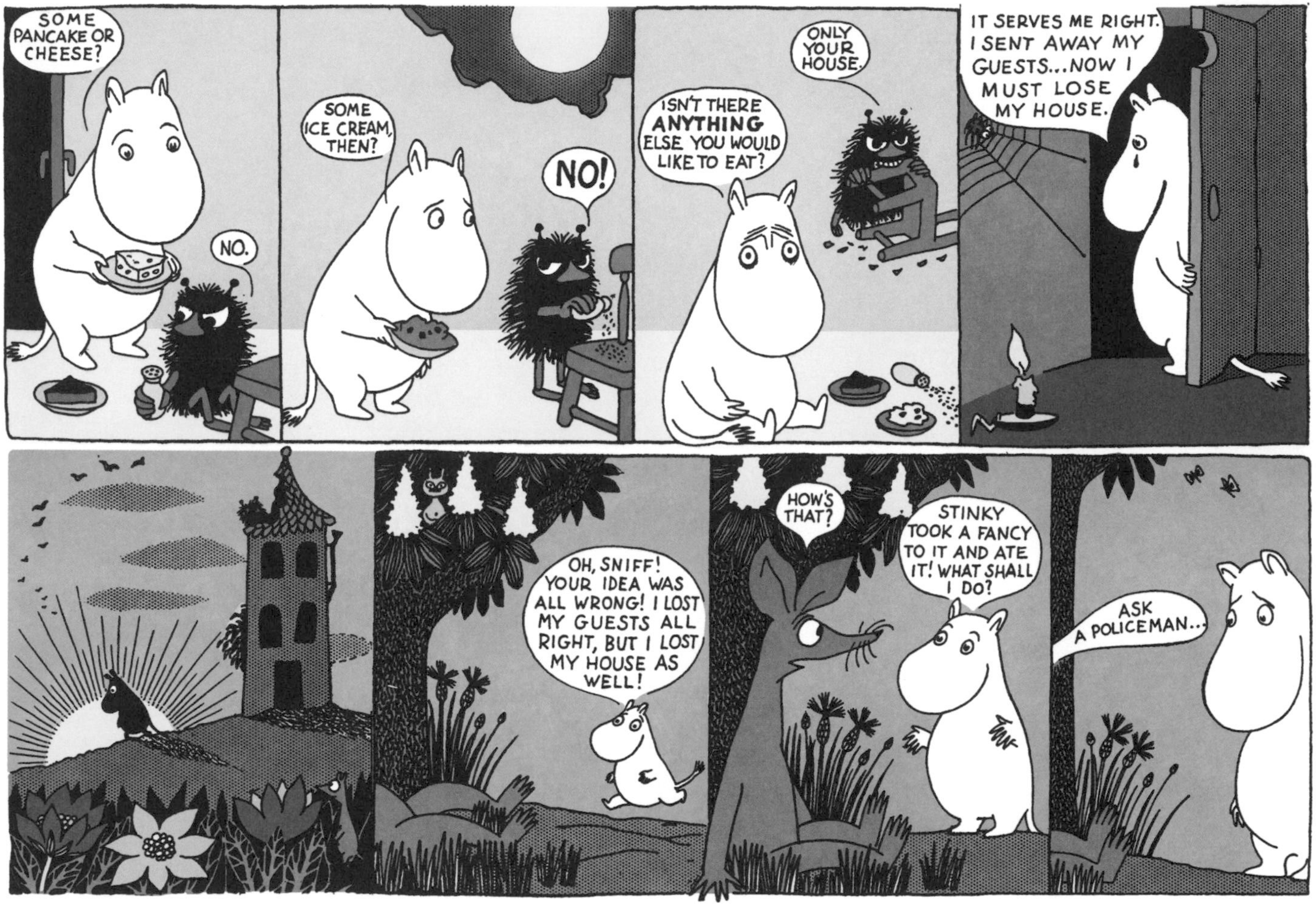
SOME PANCAKE OR CHEESE?
NO.
SOME ICE CREAM, THEN?
NO!
ISN'T THERE ANYTHING ELSE YOU WOULD LIKE TO EAT?
ONLY YOUR HOUSE.
IT SERVES ME RIGHT. I SENT AWAY MY GUESTS...NOW I MUST LOSE MY HOUSE.
OH, SNIFF! YOUR IDEA WAS ALL WRONG! I LOST MY GUESTS ALL RIGHT, BUT I LOST MY HOUSE AS WELL!
HOW'S THAT?
STINKY TOOK A FANCY TO IT AND ATE IT! WHAT SHALL I DO?
ASK A POLICEMAN...

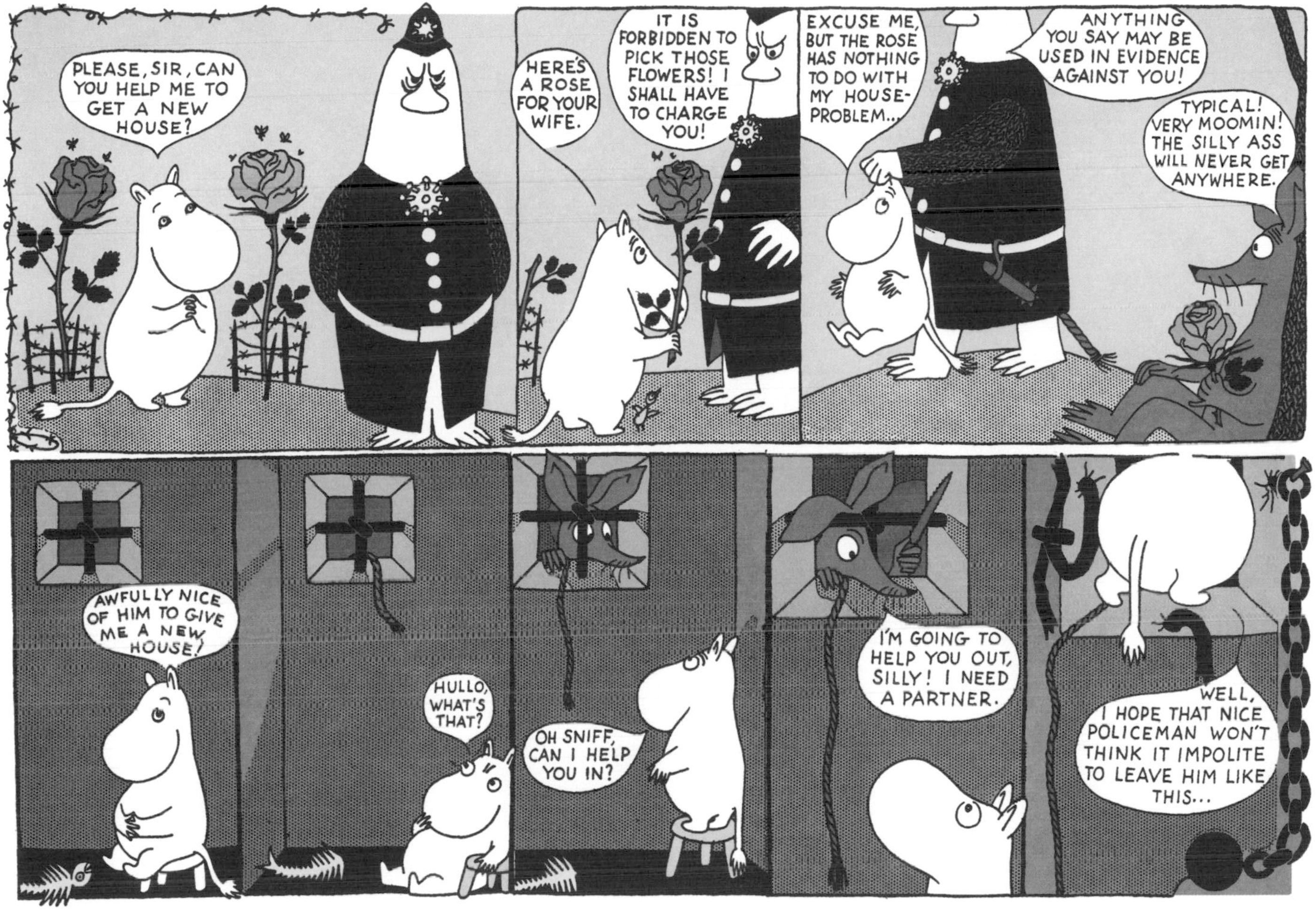
PLEASE, SIR, CAN YOU HELP ME TO GET A NEW HOUSE?
HERE'S A ROSE FOR YOUR WIFE.
IT IS FORBIDDEN TO PICK THOSE FLOWERS! I SHALL HAVE TO CHARGE YOU!
EXCUSE ME, BUT THE ROSE HAS NOTHING TO DO WITH MY HOUSE-PROBLEM...
ANYTHING YOU SAY MAY BE USED IN EVIDENCE AGAINST YOU!
TYPICAL! VERY MOOMIN! THE SILLY ASS WILL NEVER GET ANYWHERE.
AWFULLY NICE OF HIM TO GIVE ME A NEW HOUSE!
HULLO, WHAT'S THAT?
OH SNIFF, CAN I HELP YOU IN?
I'M GOING TO HELP YOU OUT, SILLY! I NEED A PARTNER.
WELL, I HOPE THAT NICE POLICEMAN WON'T THINK IT IMPOLITE TO LEAVE HIM LIKE THIS...

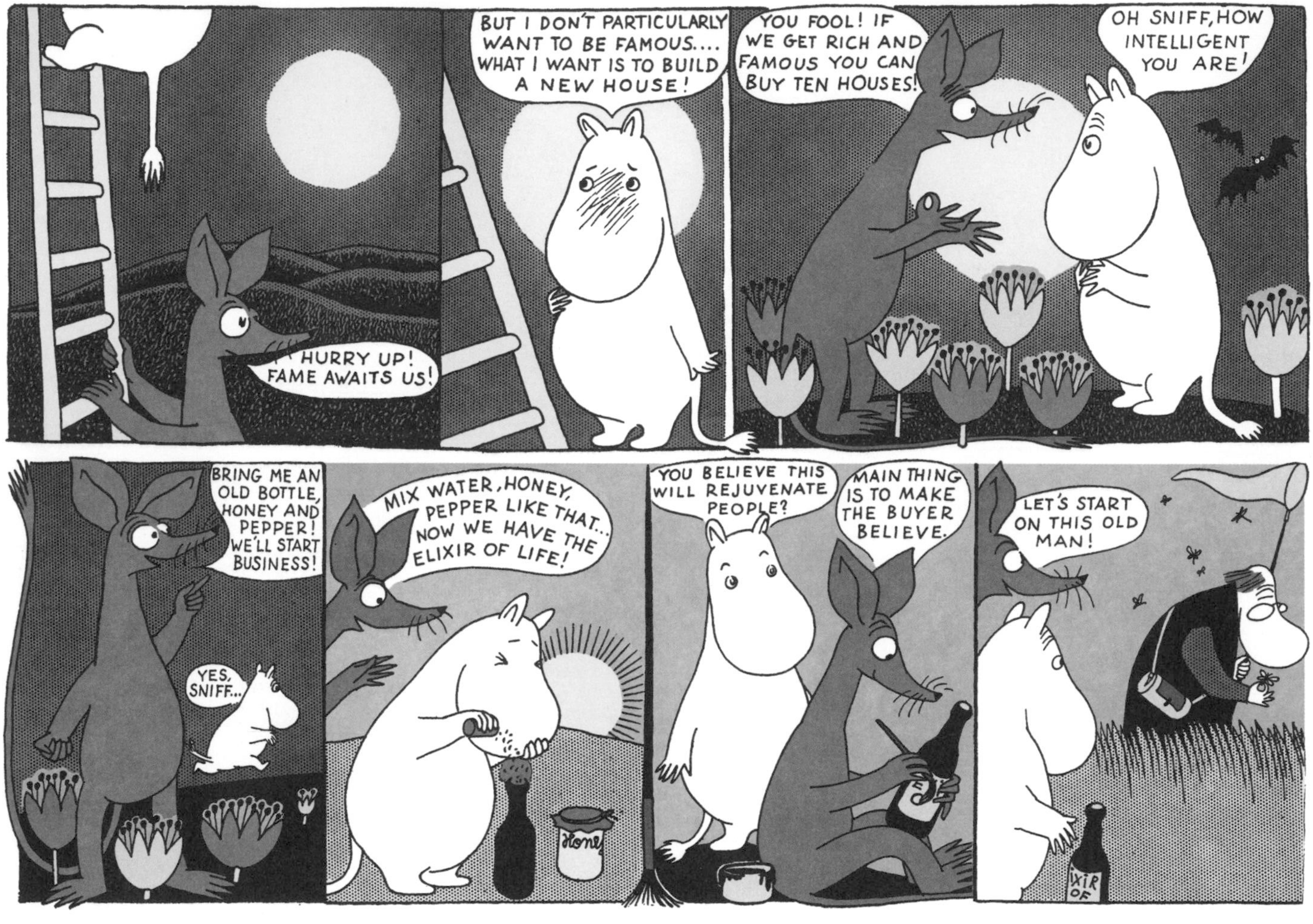
HURRY UP! FAME AWAITS US!
BUT I DON'T PARTICULARLY WANT TO BE FAMOUS.... WHAT I WANT IS TO BUILD A NEW HOUSE!
YOU FOOL! IF WE GET RICH AND FAMOUS YOU CAN BUY TEN HOUSES!
OH SNIFF, HOW INTELLIGENT YOU ARE!
BRING ME AN OLD BOTTLE, HONEY AND PEPPER! WE'LL START BUSINESS!
YES, SNIFF...
MIX WATER, HONEY, PEPPER LIKE THAT... NOW WE HAVE THE ELIXIR OF LIFE!
Honey
YOU BELIEVE THIS WILL REJUVENATE PEOPLE?
MAIN THING IS TO MAKE THE BUYER BELIEVE.
LET'S START ON THIS OLD MAN!

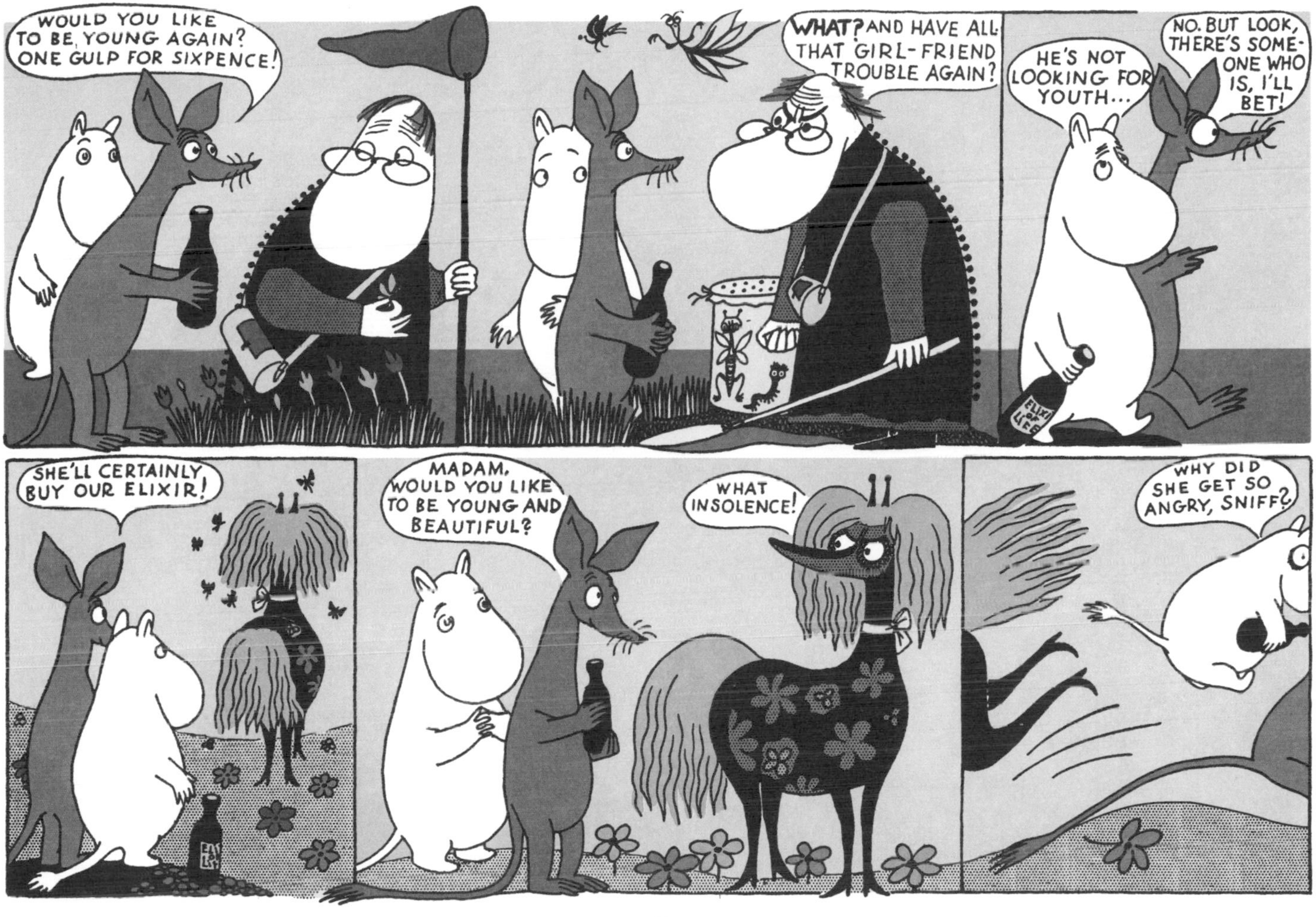
WOULD YOU LIKE TO BE YOUNG AGAIN? ONE GULP FOR SIXPENCE!
WHAT? AND HAVE ALL THAT GIRL-FRIEND TROUBLE AGAIN?
HE'S NOT LOOKING FOR YOUTH...
NO. BUT LOOK, THERE'S SOME-ONE WHO IS, I'LL BET!
SHE'LL CERTAINLY BUY OUR ELIXIR!
MADAM, WOULD YOU LIKE TO BE YOUNG AND BEAUTIFUL?
WHAT INSOLENCE!
WHY DID SHE GET SO ANGRY, SNIFF?

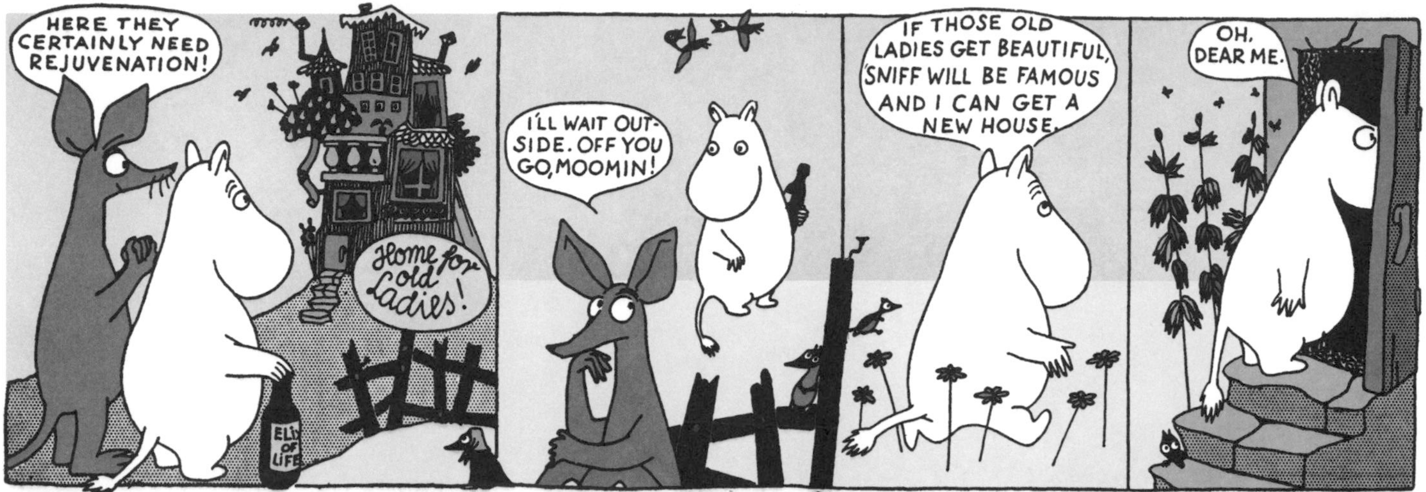
HERE THEY CERTAINLY NEED REJUVENATION!
Home for old Ladies!
ELIX OF LIFE
I'LL WAIT OUT-SIDE. OFF YOU GO, MOOMIN!
IF THOSE OLD LADIES GET BEAUTIFUL, SNIFF WILL BE FAMOUS AND I CAN GET A NEW HOUSE.
OH, DEAR ME.

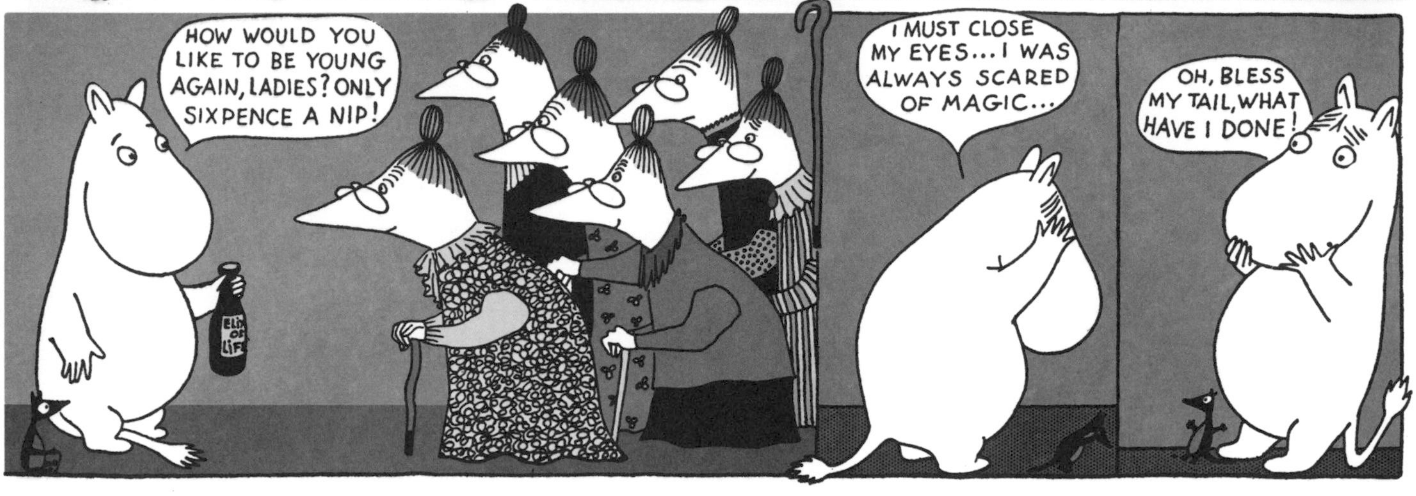
HOW WOULD YOU LIKE TO BE YOUNG AGAIN, LADIES? ONLY SIXPENCE A NIP!
I MUST CLOSE MY EYES... I WAS ALWAYS SCARED OF MAGIC...
OH, BLESS MY TAIL, WHAT HAVE I DONE!

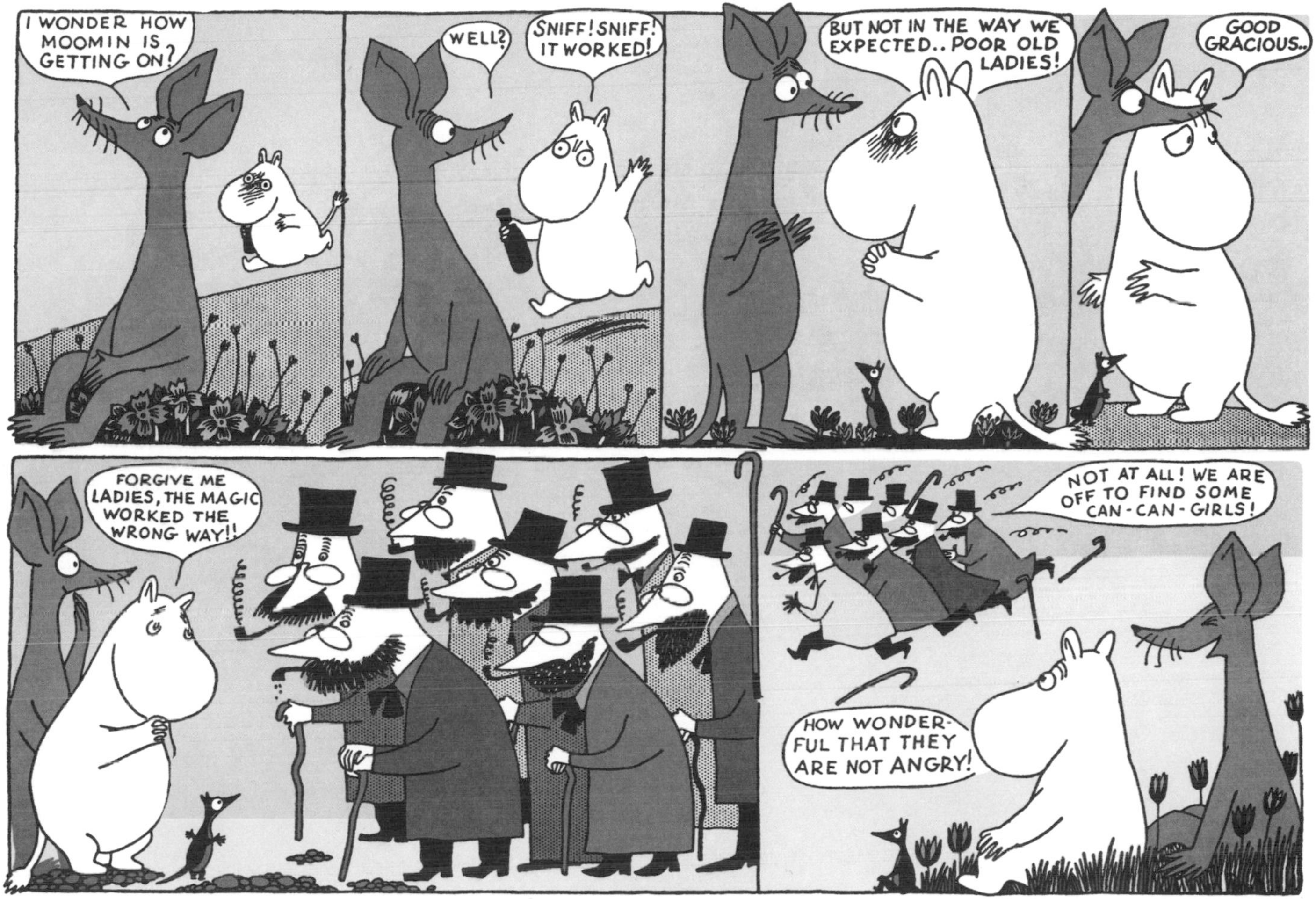
I WONDER HOW MOOMIN IS GETTING ON?
WELL?
SNIFF! SNIFF! IT WORKED!
BUT NOT IN THE WAY WE EXPECTED.. POOR OLD LADIES!
GOOD GRACIOUS..
FORGIVE ME LADIES, THE MAGIC WORKED THE WRONG WAY!!
NOT AT ALL! WE ARE OFF TO FIND SOME CAN-CAN-GIRLS!
HOW WONDERFUL THAT THEY ARE NOT ANGRY!

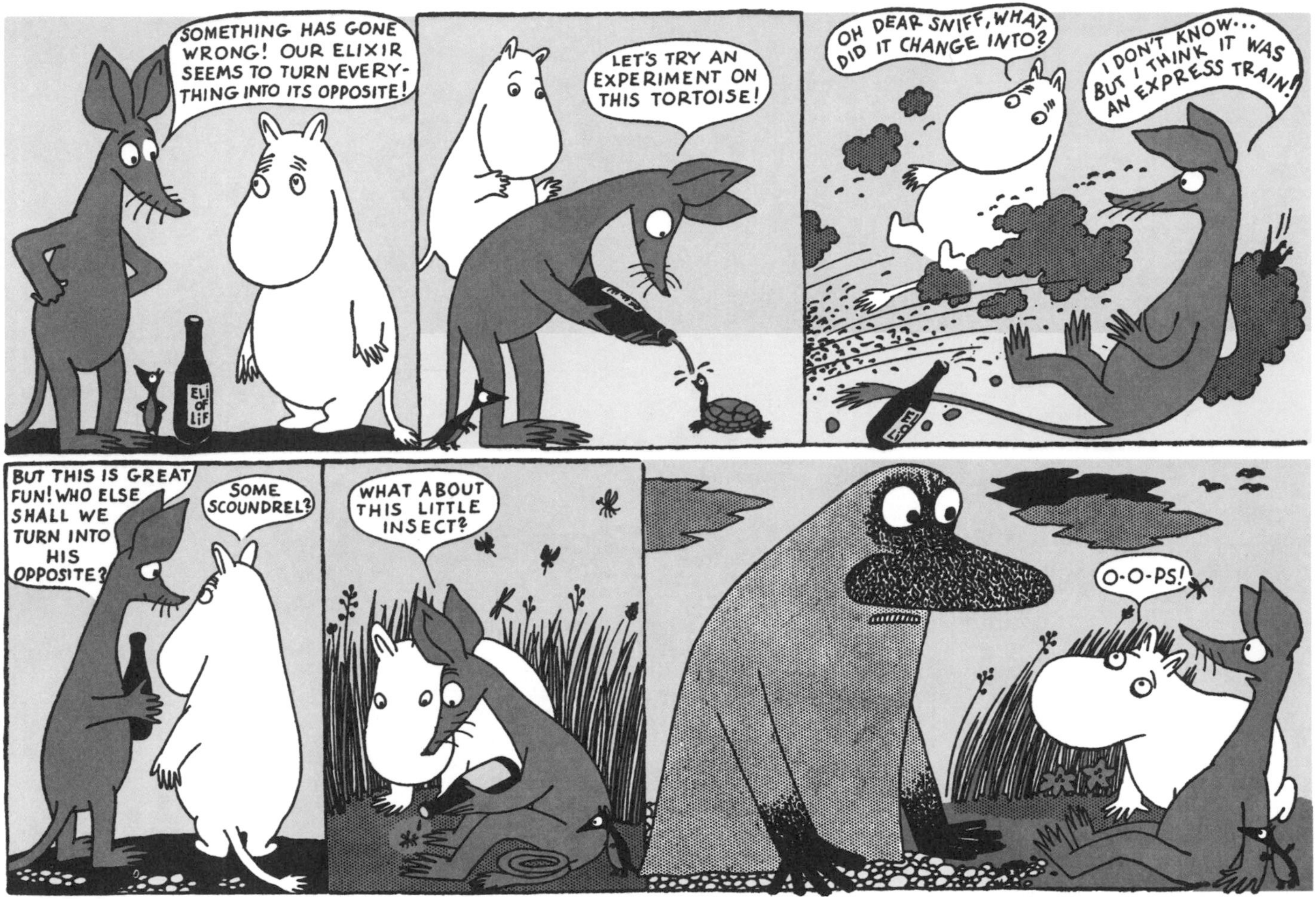
SOMETHING HAS GONE WRONG! OUR ELIXIR SEEMS TO TURN EVERY-THING INTO ITS OPPOSITE!
ELI OF LIF
LET'S TRY AN EXPERIMENT ON THIS TORTOISE!
OH DEAR SNIFF, WHAT DID IT CHANGE INTO?
I DON'T KNOW... BUT I THINK IT WAS AN EXPRESS TRAIN!
BUT THIS IS GREAT FUN! WHO ELSE SHALL WE TURN INTO HIS OPPOSITE?
SOME SCOUNDREL?
WHAT ABOUT THIS LITTLE INSECT?
O-O-PS!

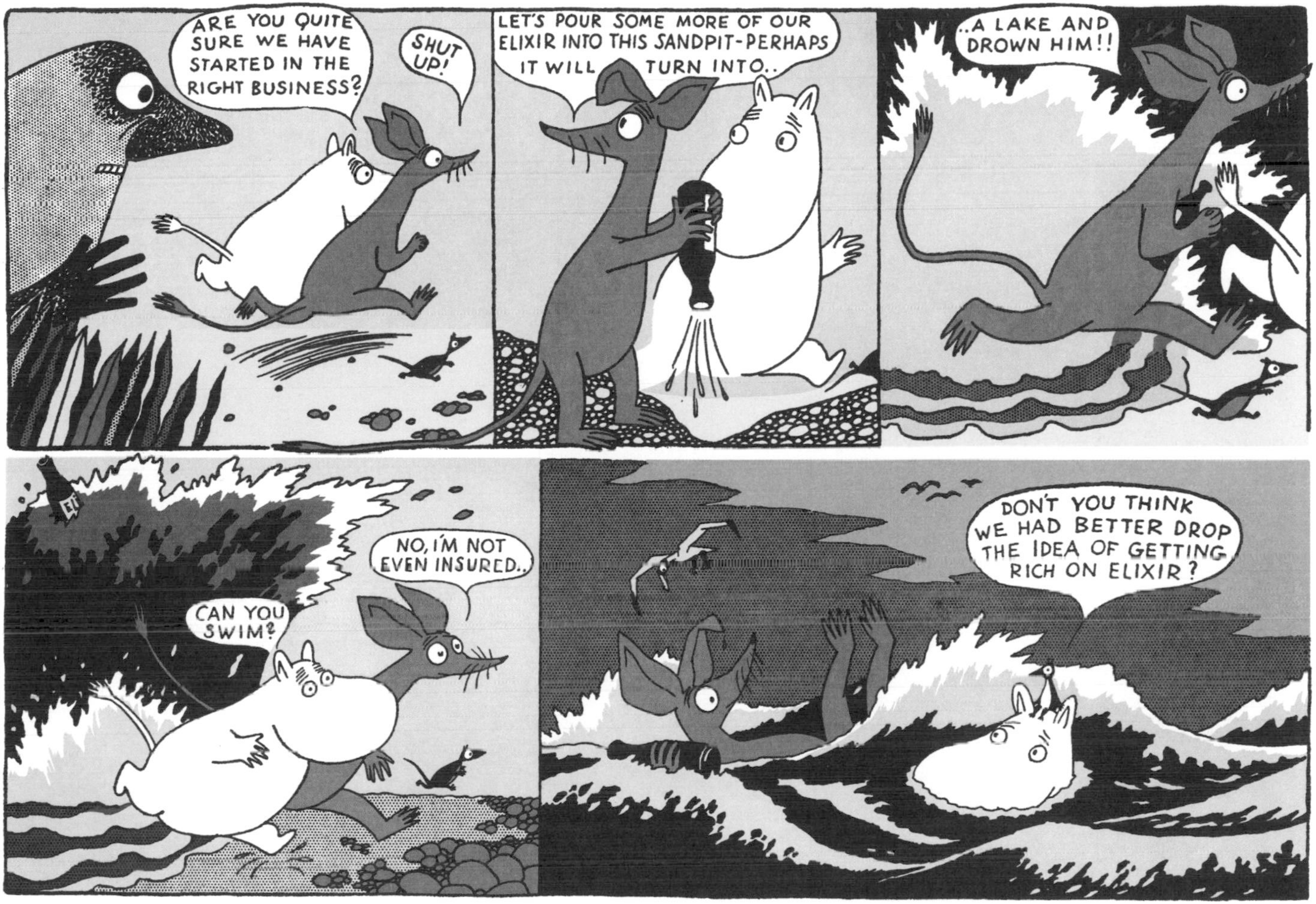
ARE YOU QUITE SURE WE HAVE STARTED IN THE RIGHT BUSINESS?
SHUT UP!
LET'S POUR SOME MORE OF OUR ELIXIR INTO THIS SANDPIT-PERHAPS IT WILL TURN INTO..
..A LAKE AND DROWN HIM!!
CAN YOU SWIM?
NO, I'M NOT EVEN INSURED..
DON'T YOU THINK WE HAD BETTER DROP THE IDEA OF GETTING RICH ON ELIXIR?

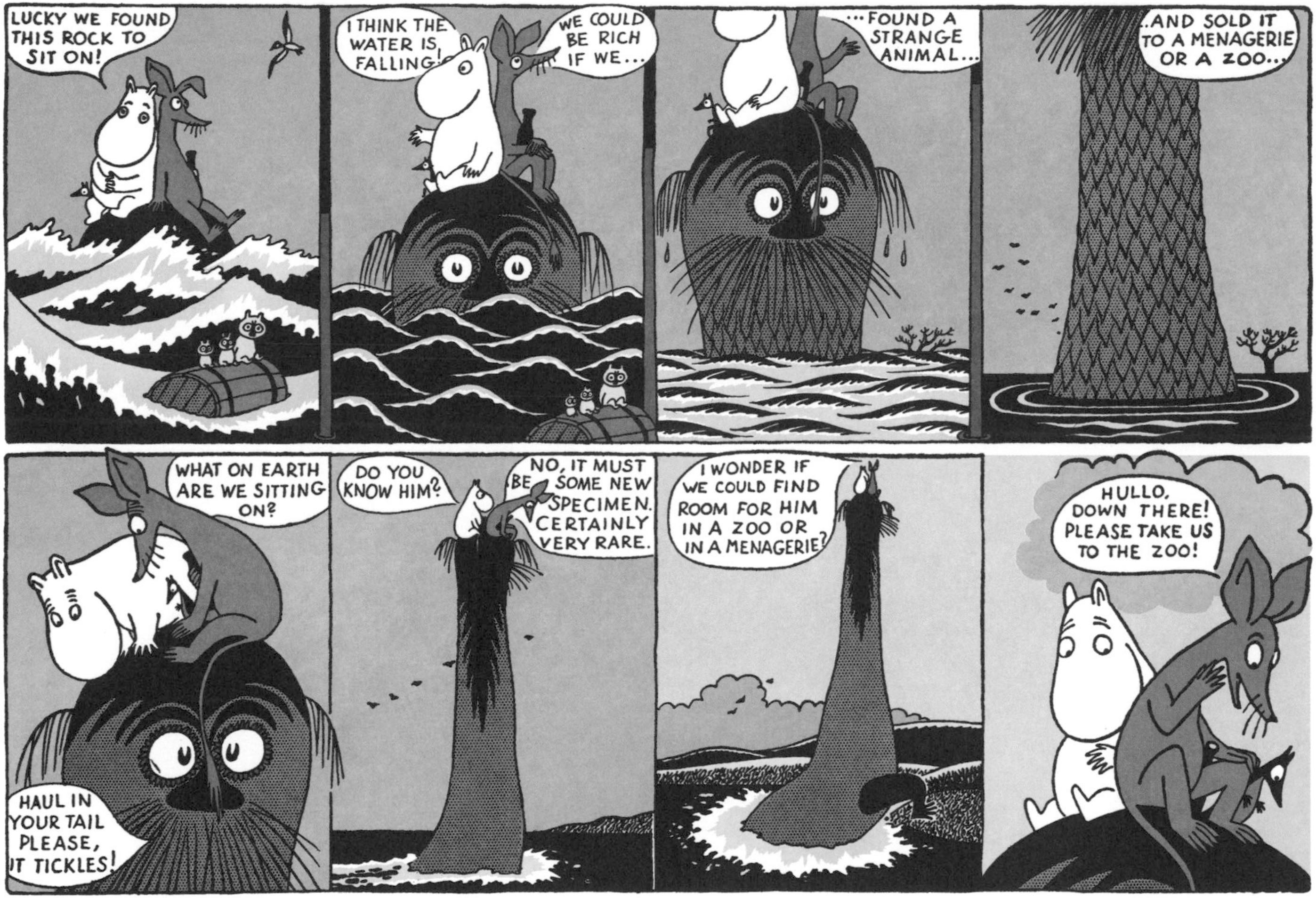
LUCKY WE FOUND THIS ROCK TO SIT ON!
I THINK THE WATER IS FALLING!
WE COULD BE RICH IF WE...
...FOUND A STRANGE ANIMAL...
..AND SOLD IT TO A MENAGERIE OR A ZOO...
WHAT ON EARTH ARE WE SITTING ON?
HAUL IN YOUR TAIL PLEASE, IT TICKLES!
DO YOU KNOW HIM?
NO, IT MUST BE SOME NEW SPECIMEN. CERTAINLY VERY RARE.
I WONDER IF WE COULD FIND ROOM FOR HIM IN A ZOO OR IN A MENAGERIE?
HULLO, DOWN THERE! PLEASE TAKE US TO THE ZOO!

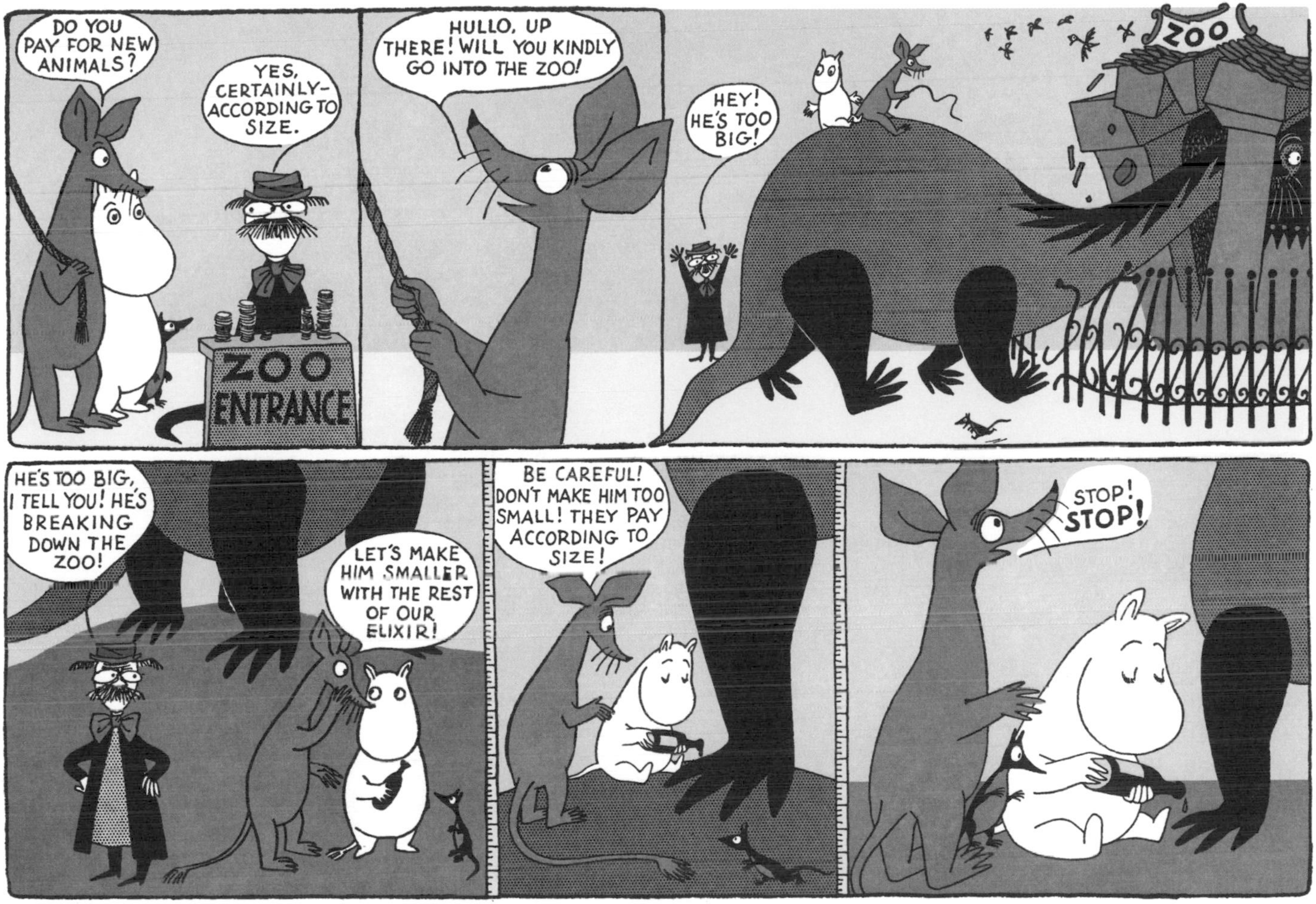
DO YOU PAY FOR NEW ANIMALS?
YES, CERTAINLY-ACCORDING TO SIZE.
ZOO ENTRANCE
HULLO, UP THERE! WILL YOU KINDLY GO INTO THE ZOO!
ZOO
HEY! HE'S TOO BIG!
HE'S TOO BIG, I TELL YOU! HE'S BREAKING DOWN THE ZOO!
LET'S MAKE HIM SMALLER WITH THE REST OF OUR ELIXIR!
BE CAREFUL! DON'T MAKE HIM TOO SMALL! THEY PAY ACCORDING TO SIZE!
STOP! STOP!

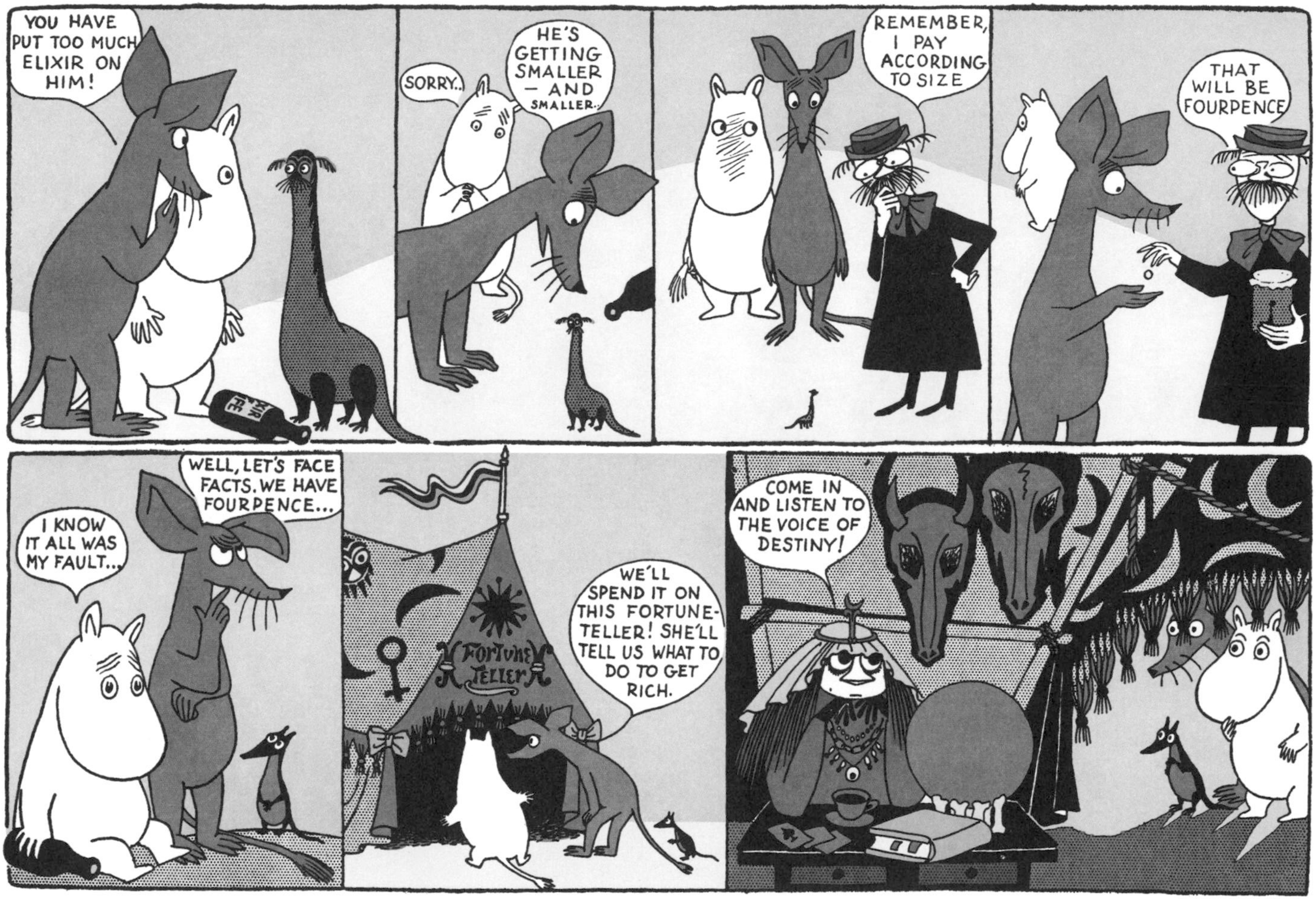
YOU HAVE PUT TOO MUCH ELIXIR ON HIM!
SORRY..
HE'S GETTING SMALLER — AND SMALLER..
REMEMBER, I PAY ACCORDING TO SIZE
THAT WILL BE FOURPENCE
I KNOW IT ALL WAS MY FAULT...
WELL, LET'S FACE FACTS. WE HAVE FOURPENCE...
FORTUNE TELLER
WE'LL SPEND IT ON THIS FORTUNE-TELLER! SHE'LL TELL US WHAT TO DO TO GET RICH.
COME IN AND LISTEN TO THE VOICE OF DESTINY!

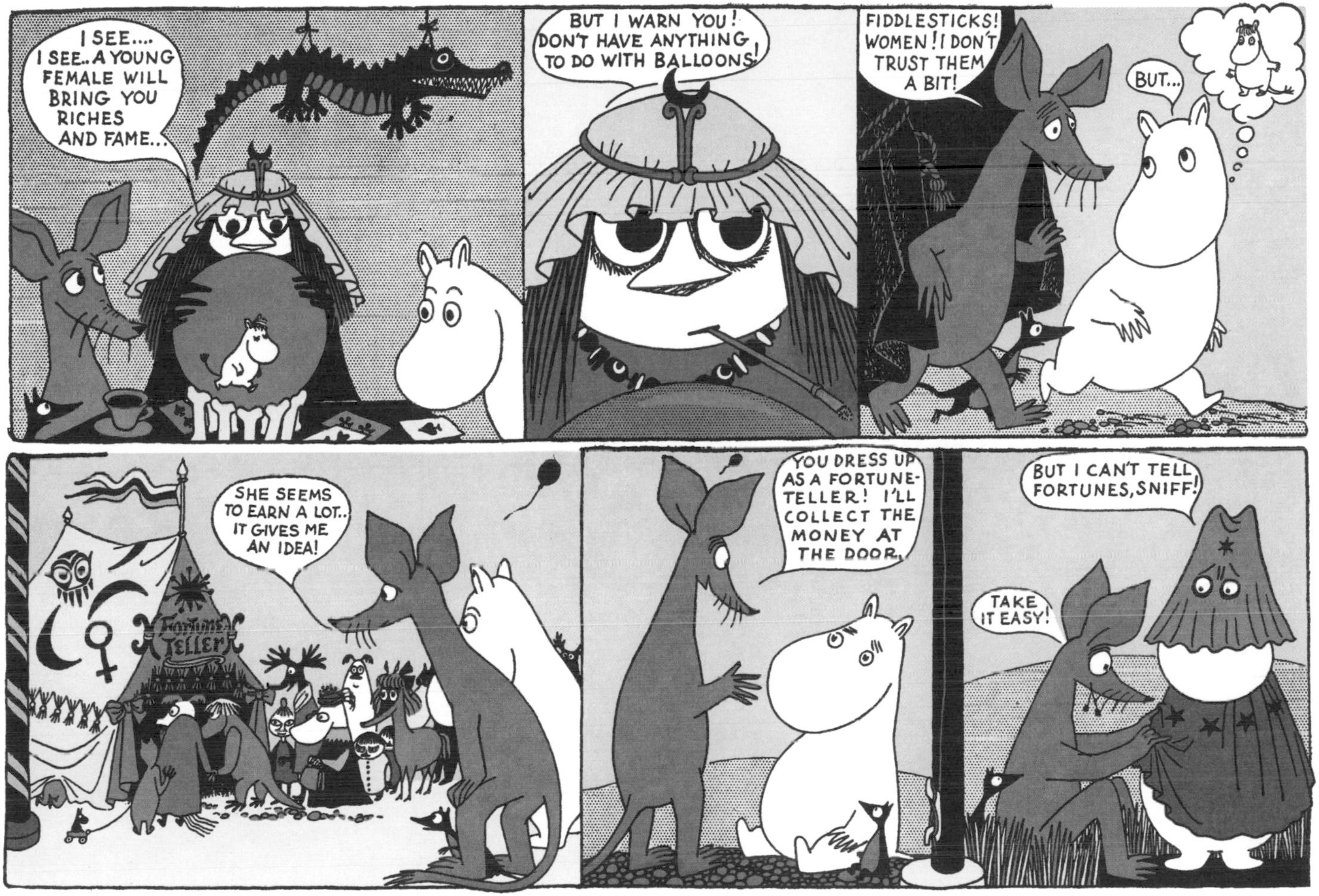

I SEE.... I SEE.. A YOUNG FEMALE WILL BRING YOU RICHES AND FAME...
BUT I WARN YOU! DON'T HAVE ANYTHING TO DO WITH BALLOONS!
FIDDLESTICKS! WOMEN! I DON'T TRUST THEM A BIT!
BUT...
SHE SEEMS TO EARN A LOT.. IT GIVES ME AN IDEA!
FORTUNE TELLER
YOU DRESS UP AS A FORTUNE-TELLER! I'LL COLLECT THE MONEY AT THE DOOR.
BUT I CAN'T TELL FORTUNES, SNIFF!
TAKE IT EASY!

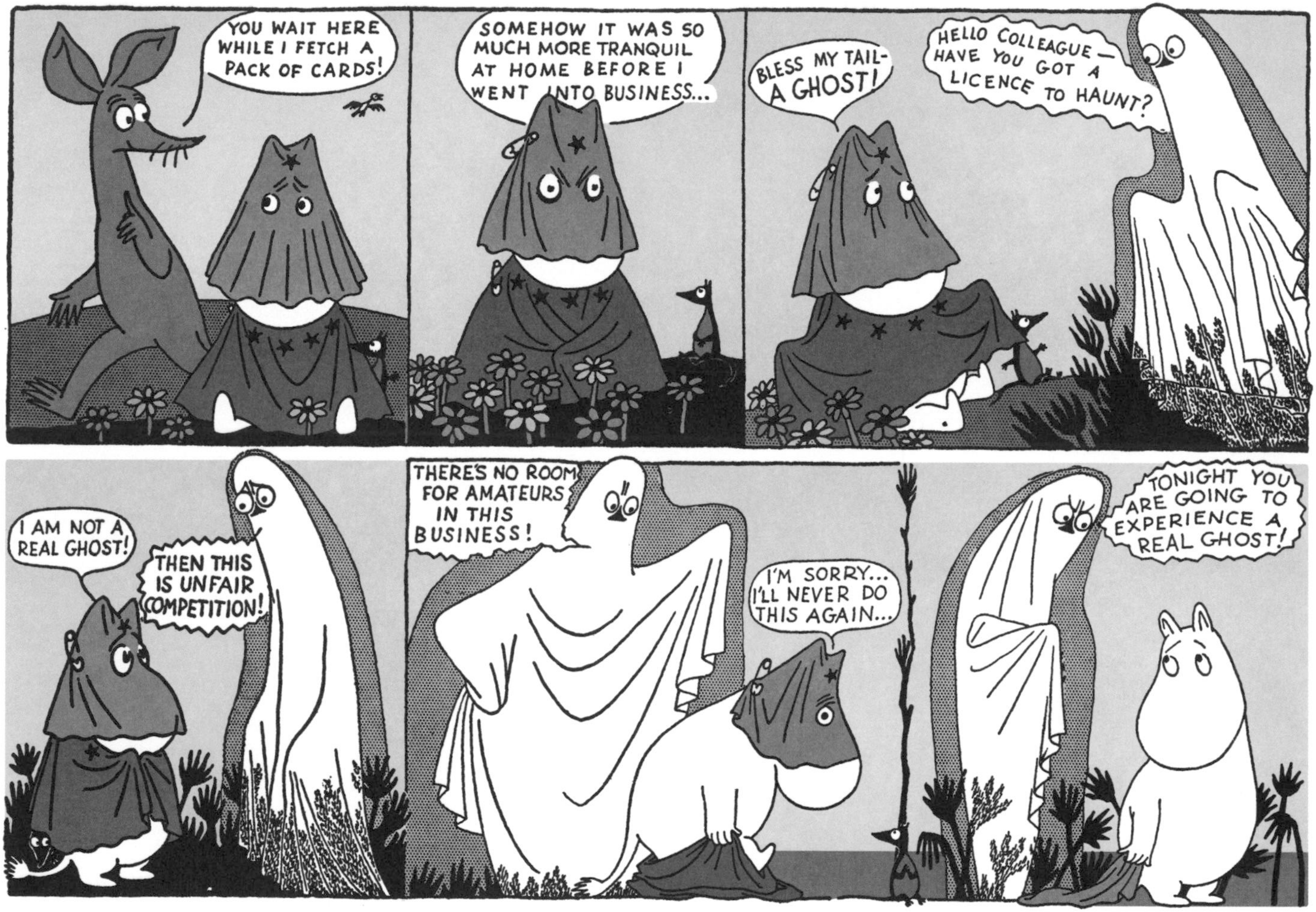
YOU WAIT HERE WHILE I FETCH A PACK OF CARDS!
SOMEHOW IT WAS SO MUCH MORE TRANQUIL AT HOME BEFORE I WENT INTO BUSINESS...
BLESS MY TAIL- A GHOST!
HELLO COLLEAGUE— HAVE YOU GOT A LICENCE TO HAUNT?
I AM NOT A REAL GHOST!
THEN THIS IS UNFAIR COMPETITION!
THERE'S NO ROOM FOR AMATEURS IN THIS BUSINESS!
I'M SORRY... I'LL NEVER DO THIS AGAIN...
TONIGHT YOU ARE GOING TO EXPERIENCE A REAL GHOST!

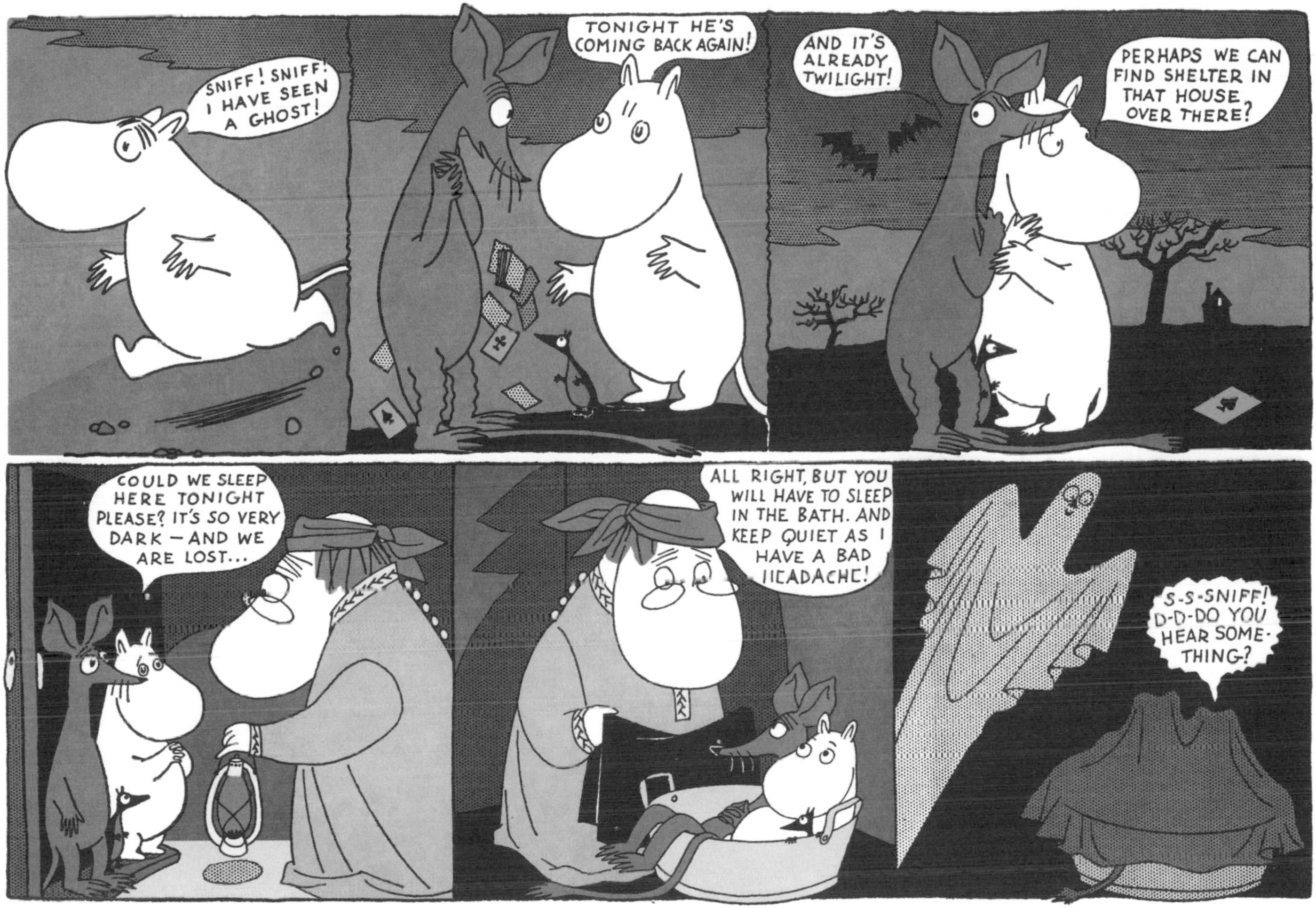
SNIFF! SNIFF! I HAVE SEEN A GHOST!
TONIGHT HE'S COMING BACK AGAIN!
AND IT'S ALREADY TWILIGHT!
PERHAPS WE CAN FIND SHELTER IN THAT HOUSE OVER THERE?
COULD WE SLEEP HERE TONIGHT PLEASE? IT'S SO VERY DARK – AND WE ARE LOST...
ALL RIGHT, BUT YOU WILL HAVE TO SLEEP IN THE BATH. AND KEEP QUIET AS I HAVE A BAD HEADACHE!
S-S-SNIFF! D-D-DO YOU HEAR SOME-THING?

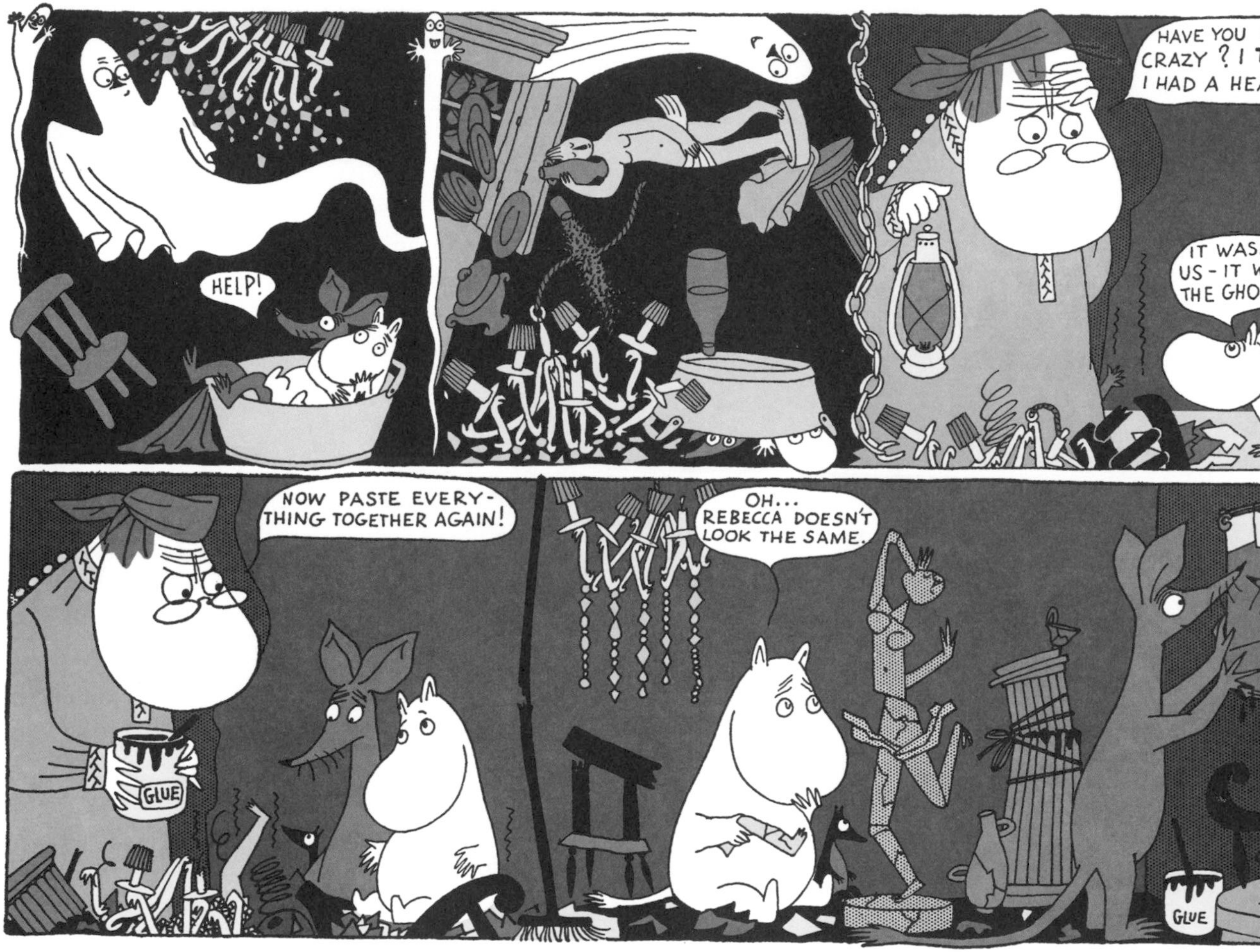
HELP!
HAVE YOU GONE CRAZY ? I **TOLD** YOU I HAD A HEADACHE!
IT WASN'T US - IT WAS THE GHOST!
NOW PASTE EVERY-THING TOGETHER AGAIN!
GLUE
OH... REBECCA DOESN'T LOOK THE SAME.
GLUE

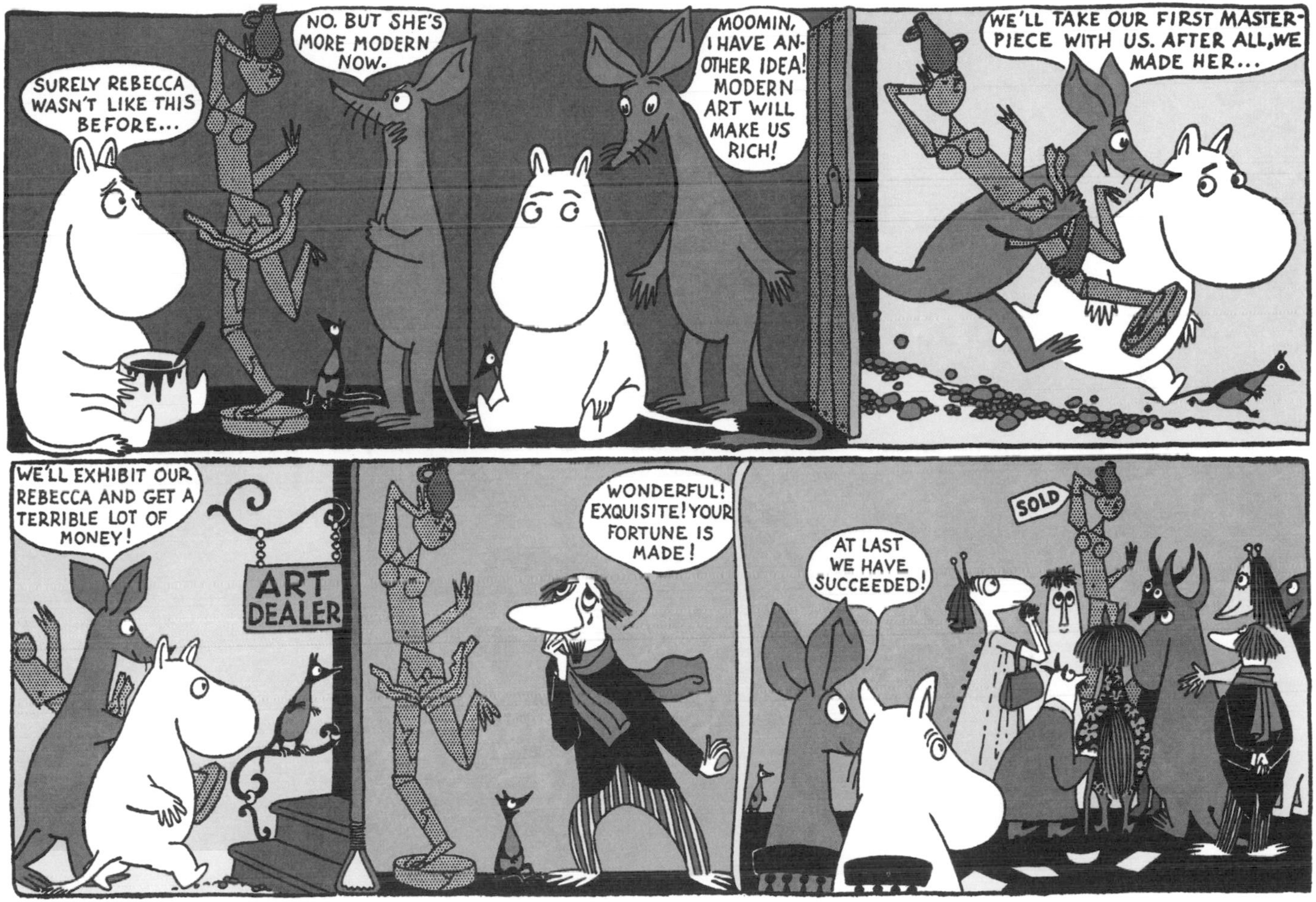
SURELY REBECCA WASN'T LIKE THIS BEFORE...
NO. BUT SHE'S MORE MODERN NOW.
MOOMIN, I HAVE AN-OTHER IDEA! MODERN ART WILL MAKE US RICH!
WE'LL TAKE OUR FIRST MASTER-PIECE WITH US. AFTER ALL, WE MADE HER...
WE'LL EXHIBIT OUR REBECCA AND GET A TERRIBLE LOT OF MONEY!
ART DEALER
WONDERFUL! EXQUISITE! YOUR FORTUNE IS MADE!
SOLD
AT LAST WE HAVE SUCCEEDED!

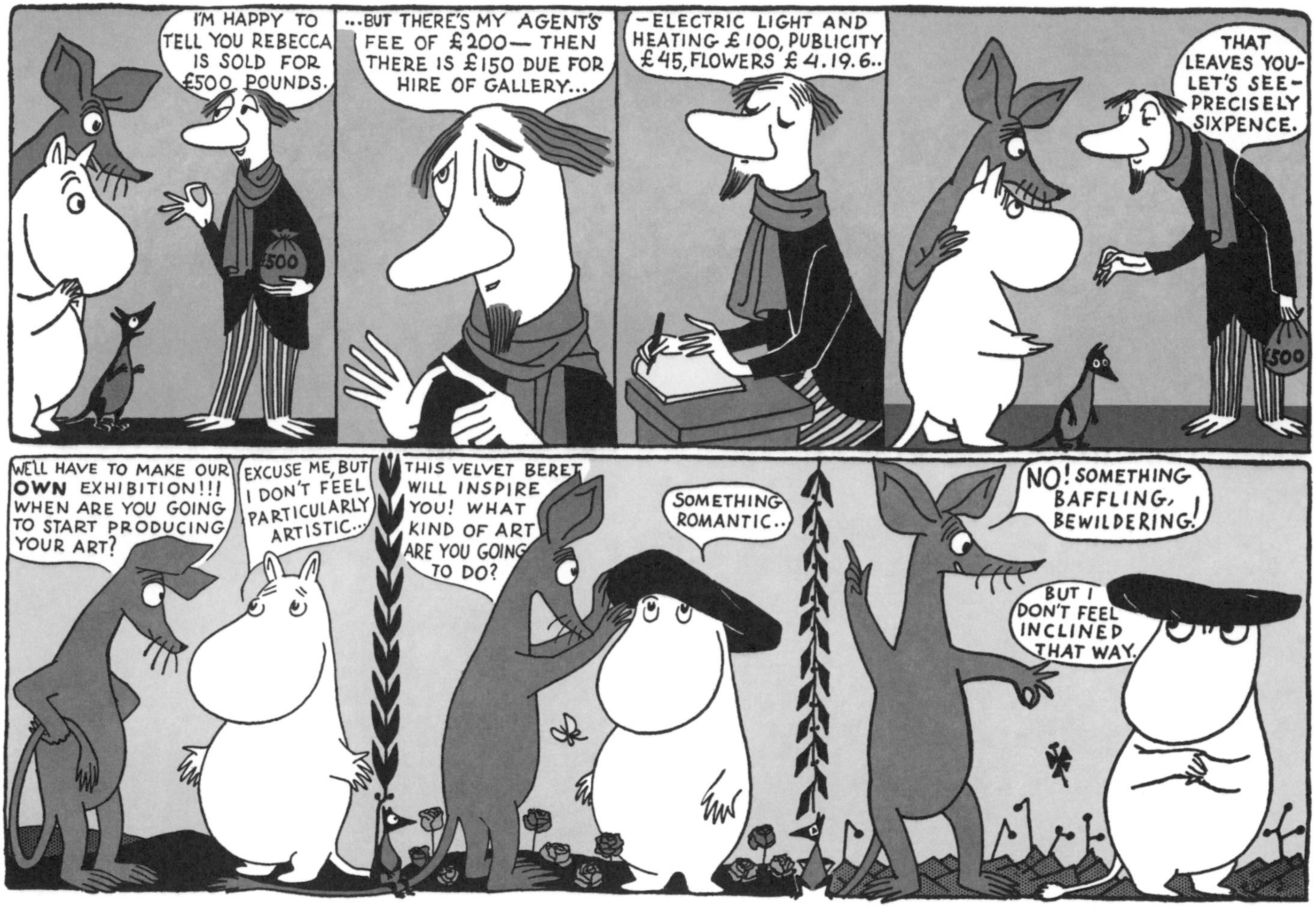
I'M HAPPY TO TELL YOU REBECCA IS SOLD FOR £500 POUNDS.
£500
...BUT THERE'S MY AGENT'S FEE OF £200— THEN THERE IS £150 DUE FOR HIRE OF GALLERY...
—ELECTRIC LIGHT AND HEATING £100, PUBLICITY £45, FLOWERS £4.19.6..
THAT LEAVES YOU— LET'S SEE— PRECISELY SIXPENCE.
£500
WE'LL HAVE TO MAKE OUR OWN EXHIBITION!!! WHEN ARE YOU GOING TO START PRODUCING YOUR ART?
EXCUSE ME, BUT I DON'T FEEL PARTICULARLY ARTISTIC...
THIS VELVET BERET WILL INSPIRE YOU! WHAT KIND OF ART ARE YOU GOING TO DO?
SOMETHING ROMANTIC...
NO! SOMETHING BAFFLING, BEWILDERING!
BUT I DON'T FEEL INCLINED THAT WAY.

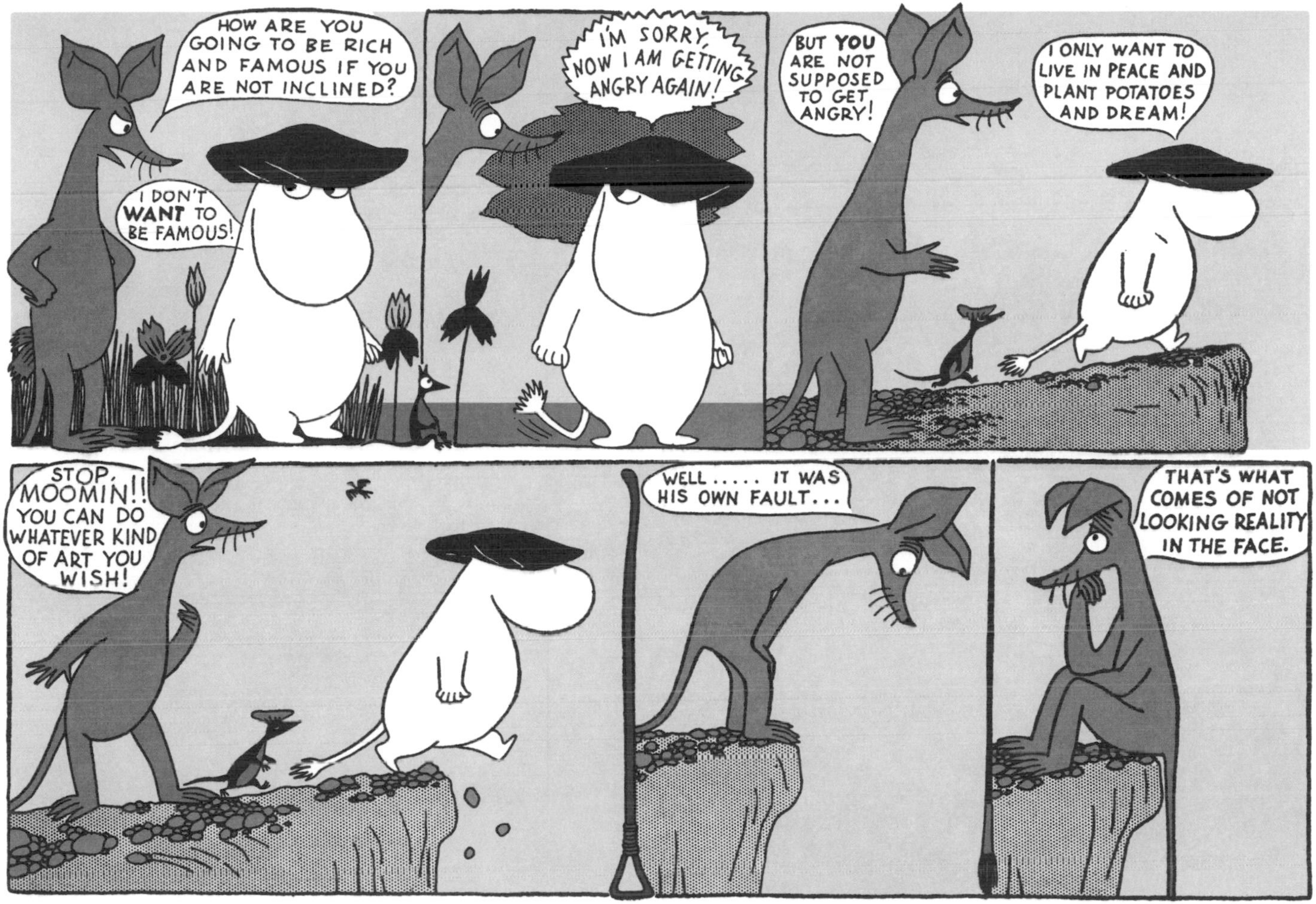
HOW ARE YOU GOING TO BE RICH AND FAMOUS IF YOU ARE NOT INCLINED?
I DON'T **WANT** TO BE FAMOUS!
I'M SORRY, NOW I AM GETTING ANGRY AGAIN!
BUT **YOU** ARE NOT SUPPOSED TO GET ANGRY!
I ONLY WANT TO LIVE IN PEACE AND PLANT POTATOES AND DREAM!
STOP, MOOMIN!! YOU CAN DO WHATEVER KIND OF ART YOU WISH!
WELL ..... IT WAS HIS OWN FAULT...
THAT'S WHAT COMES OF NOT LOOKING REALITY IN THE FACE.

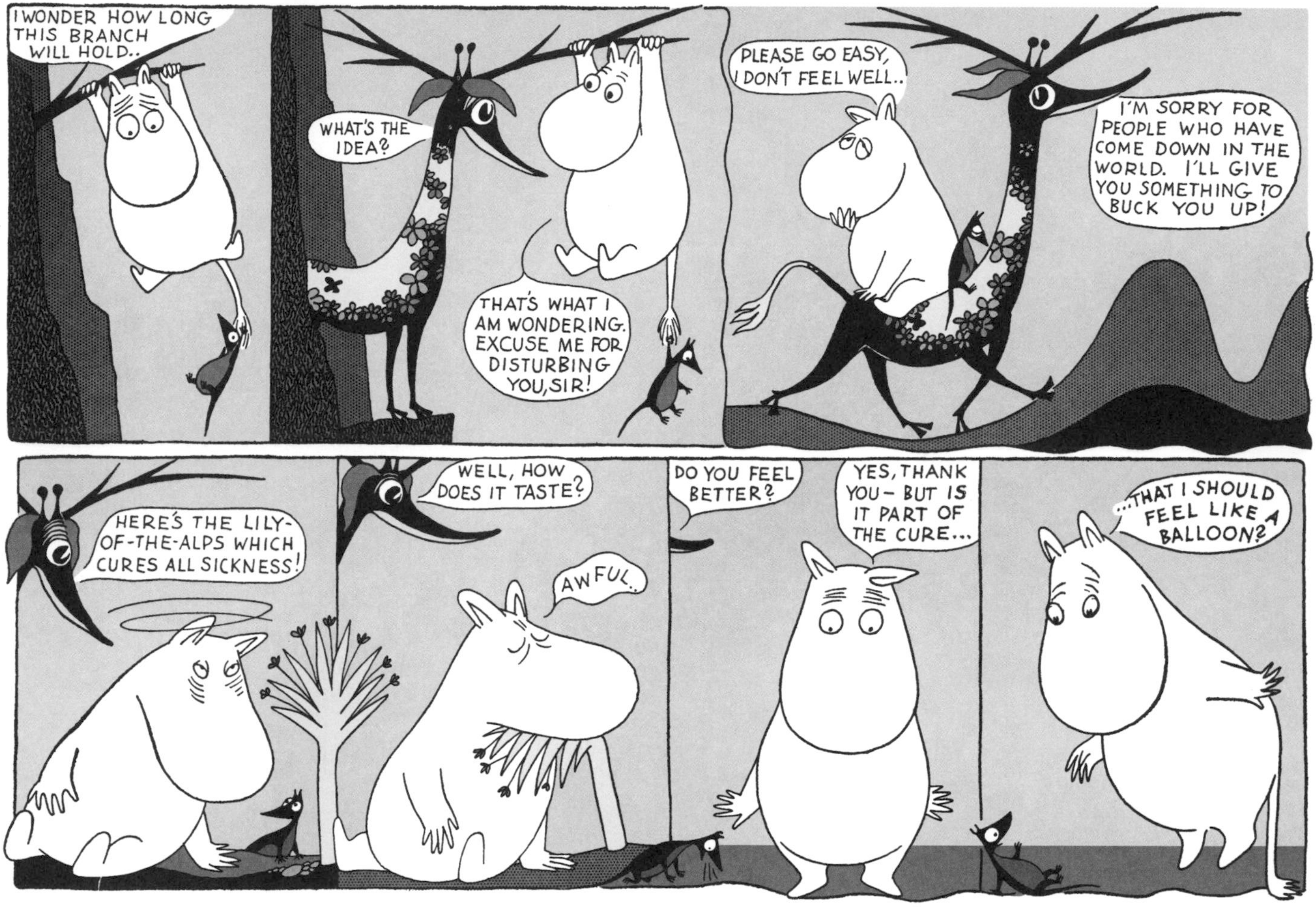
I WONDER HOW LONG THIS BRANCH WILL HOLD..
WHAT'S THE IDEA?
THAT'S WHAT I AM WONDERING. EXCUSE ME FOR DISTURBING YOU, SIR!
PLEASE GO EASY, I DON'T FEEL WELL..
I'M SORRY FOR PEOPLE WHO HAVE COME DOWN IN THE WORLD. I'LL GIVE YOU SOMETHING TO BUCK YOU UP!
HERE'S THE LILY-OF-THE-ALPS WHICH CURES ALL SICKNESS!
WELL, HOW DOES IT TASTE?
AWFUL..
DO YOU FEEL BETTER?
YES, THANK YOU – BUT IS IT PART OF THE CURE...
...THAT I SHOULD FEEL LIKE A BALLOON?

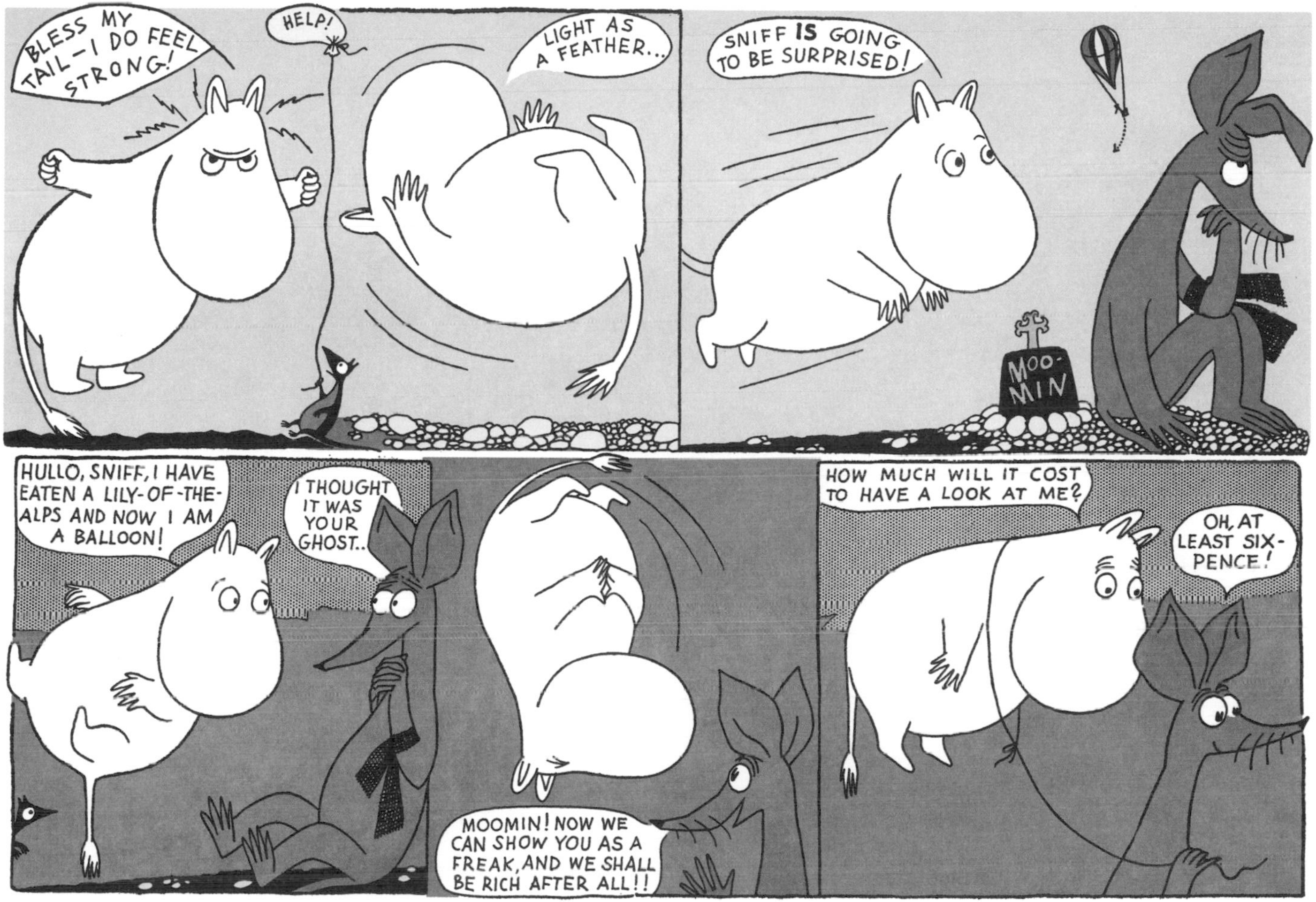
BLESS MY TAIL—I DO FEEL STRONG!
HELP!
LIGHT AS A FEATHER...
SNIFF IS GOING TO BE SURPRISED!
MOO-MIN
HULLO, SNIFF, I HAVE EATEN A LILY-OF-THE-ALPS AND NOW I AM A BALLOON!
I THOUGHT IT WAS YOUR GHOST..
MOOMIN! NOW WE CAN SHOW YOU AS A FREAK, AND WE SHALL BE RICH AFTER ALL!!
HOW MUCH WILL IT COST TO HAVE A LOOK AT ME?
OH, AT LEAST SIX-PENCE!

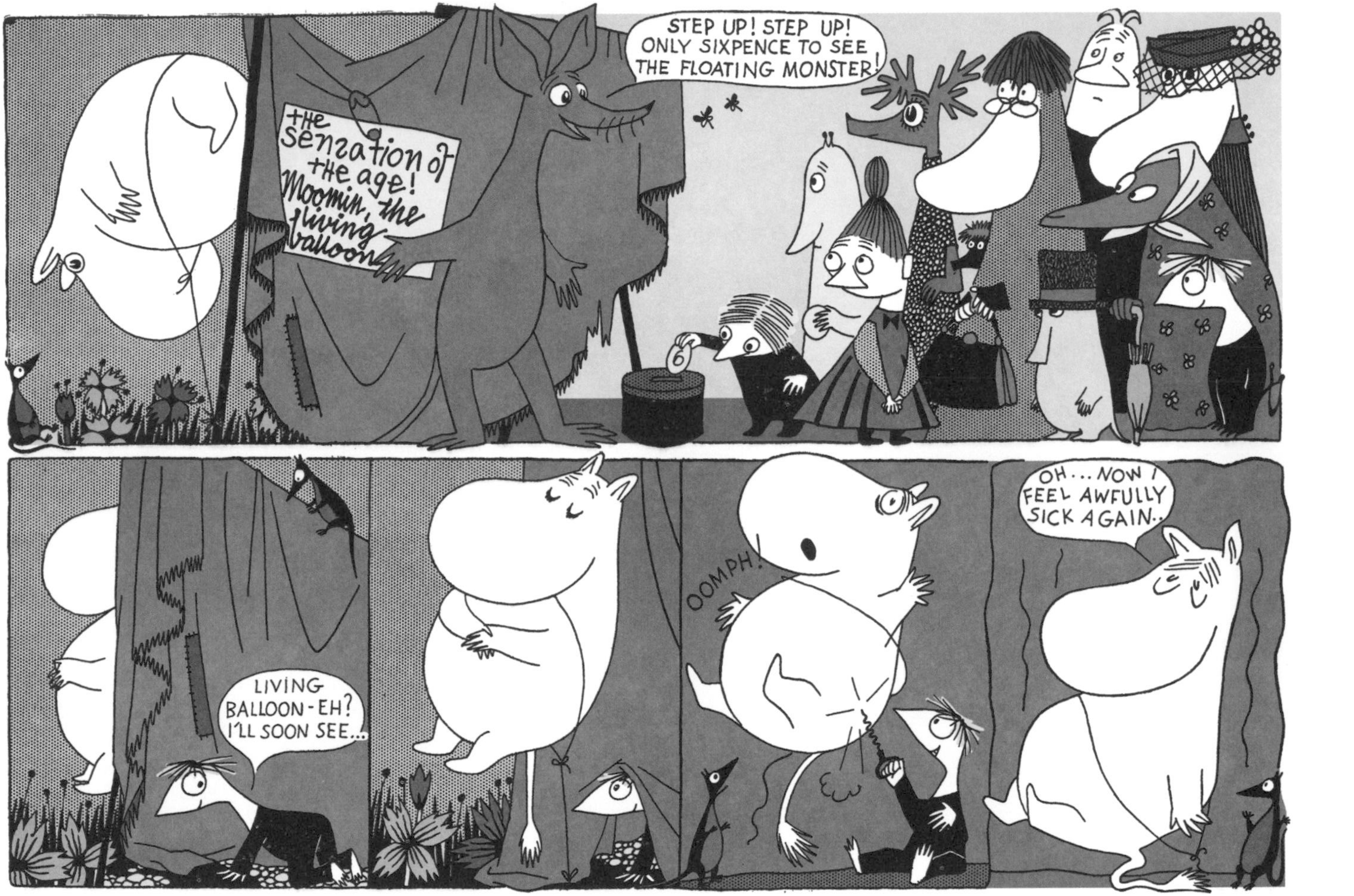
the senzation of the age! Moomin, the living balloon
STEP UP! STEP UP! ONLY SIXPENCE TO SEE THE FLOATING MONSTER!
LIVING BALLOON-EH? I'LL SOON SEE...
OOMPH!
OH... NOW I FEEL AWFULLY SICK AGAIN..

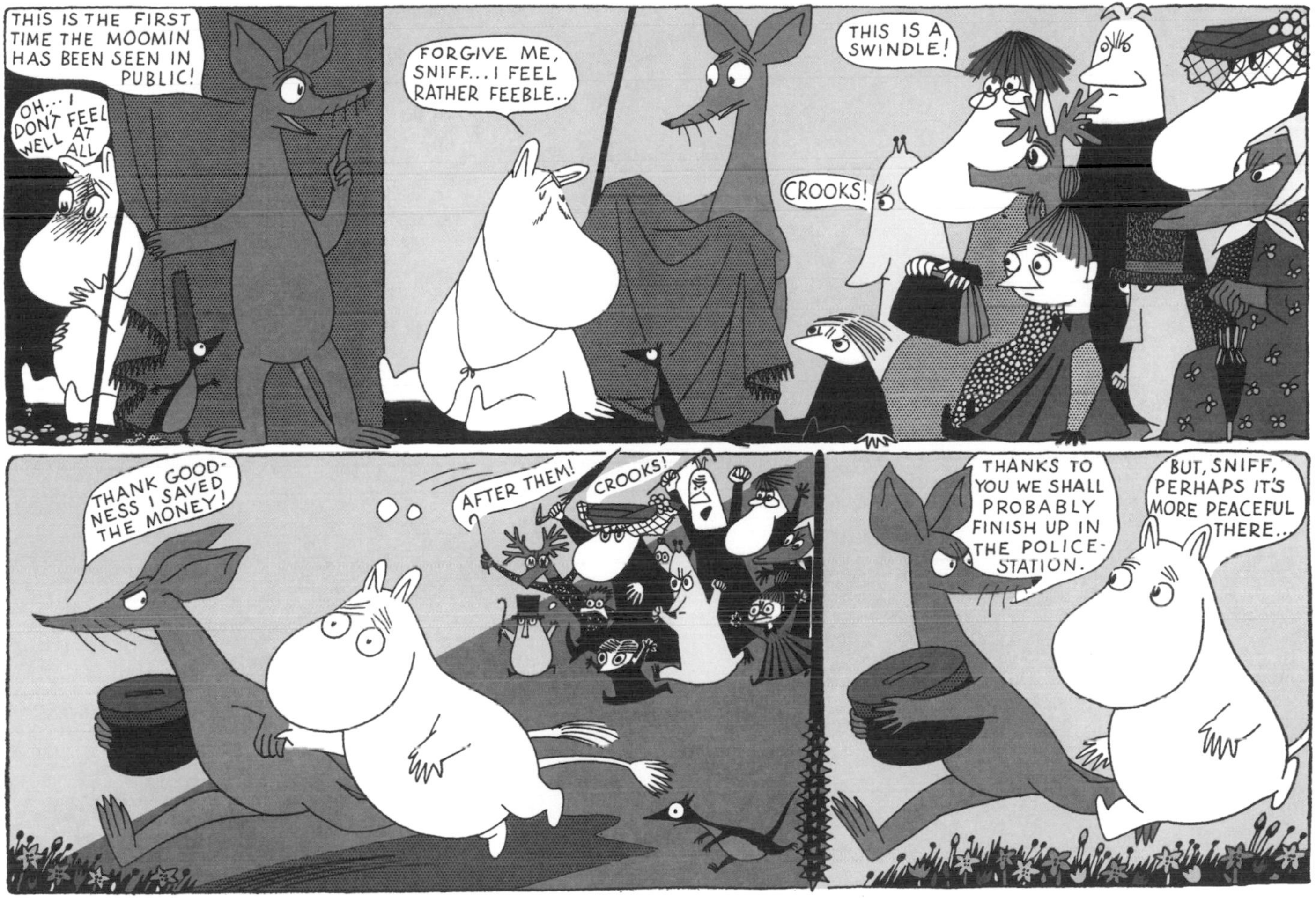
THIS IS THE FIRST TIME THE MOOMIN HAS BEEN SEEN IN PUBLIC!
OH... I DON'T FEEL WELL AT ALL
FORGIVE ME, SNIFF... I FEEL RATHER FEEBLE..
THIS IS A SWINDLE!
CROOKS!
THANK GOODNESS I SAVED THE MONEY!
AFTER THEM!
CROOKS!
THANKS TO YOU WE SHALL PROBABLY FINISH UP IN THE POLICE-STATION.
BUT, SNIFF, PERHAPS IT'S MORE PEACEFUL THERE...

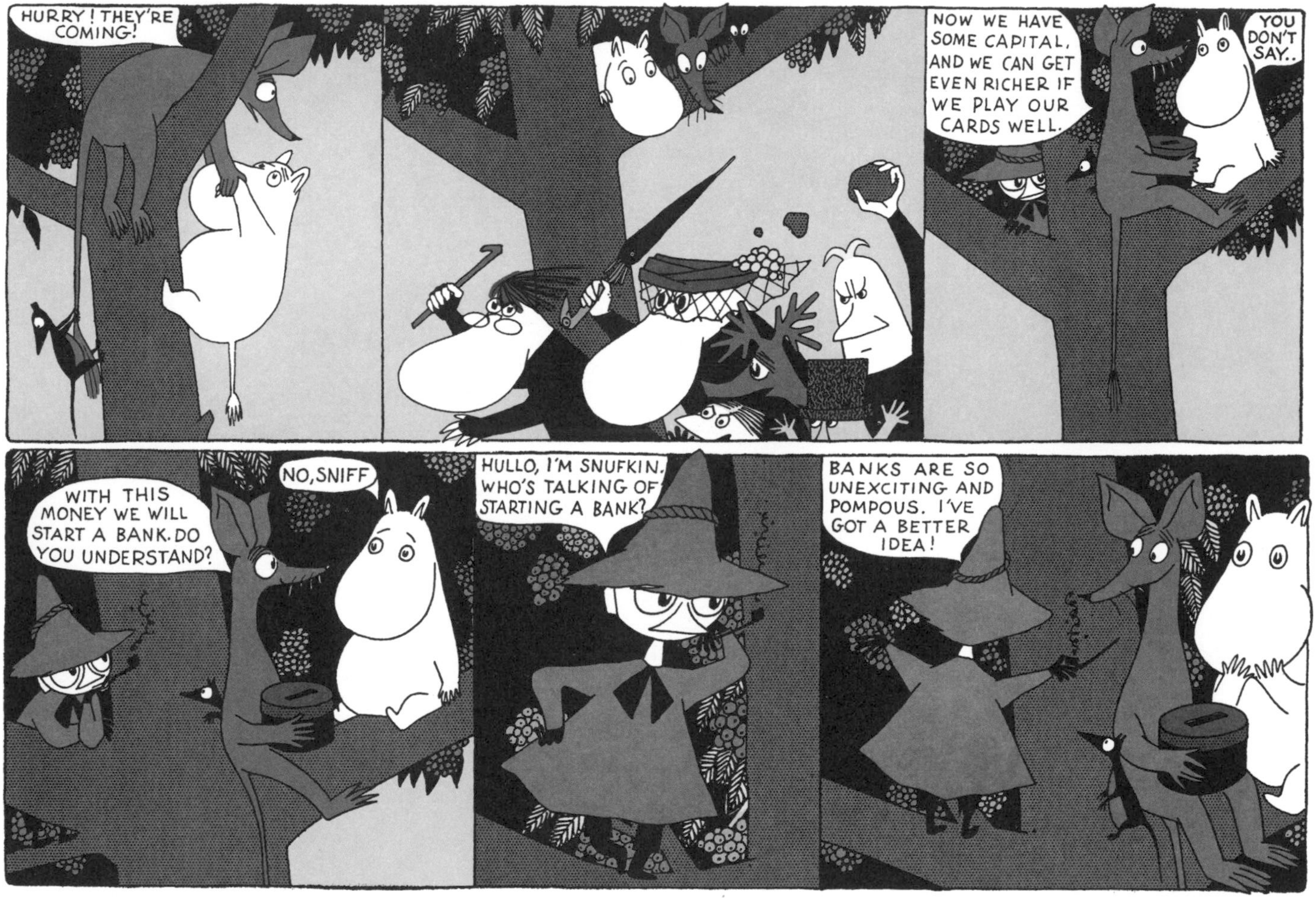
HURRY! THEY'RE COMING!
NOW WE HAVE SOME CAPITAL, AND WE CAN GET EVEN RICHER IF WE PLAY OUR CARDS WELL.
YOU DON'T SAY..
WITH THIS MONEY WE WILL START A BANK. DO YOU UNDERSTAND?
NO, SNIFF
HULLO, I'M SNUFKIN. WHO'S TALKING OF STARTING A BANK?
BANKS ARE SO UNEXCITING AND POMPOUS. I'VE GOT A BETTER IDEA!

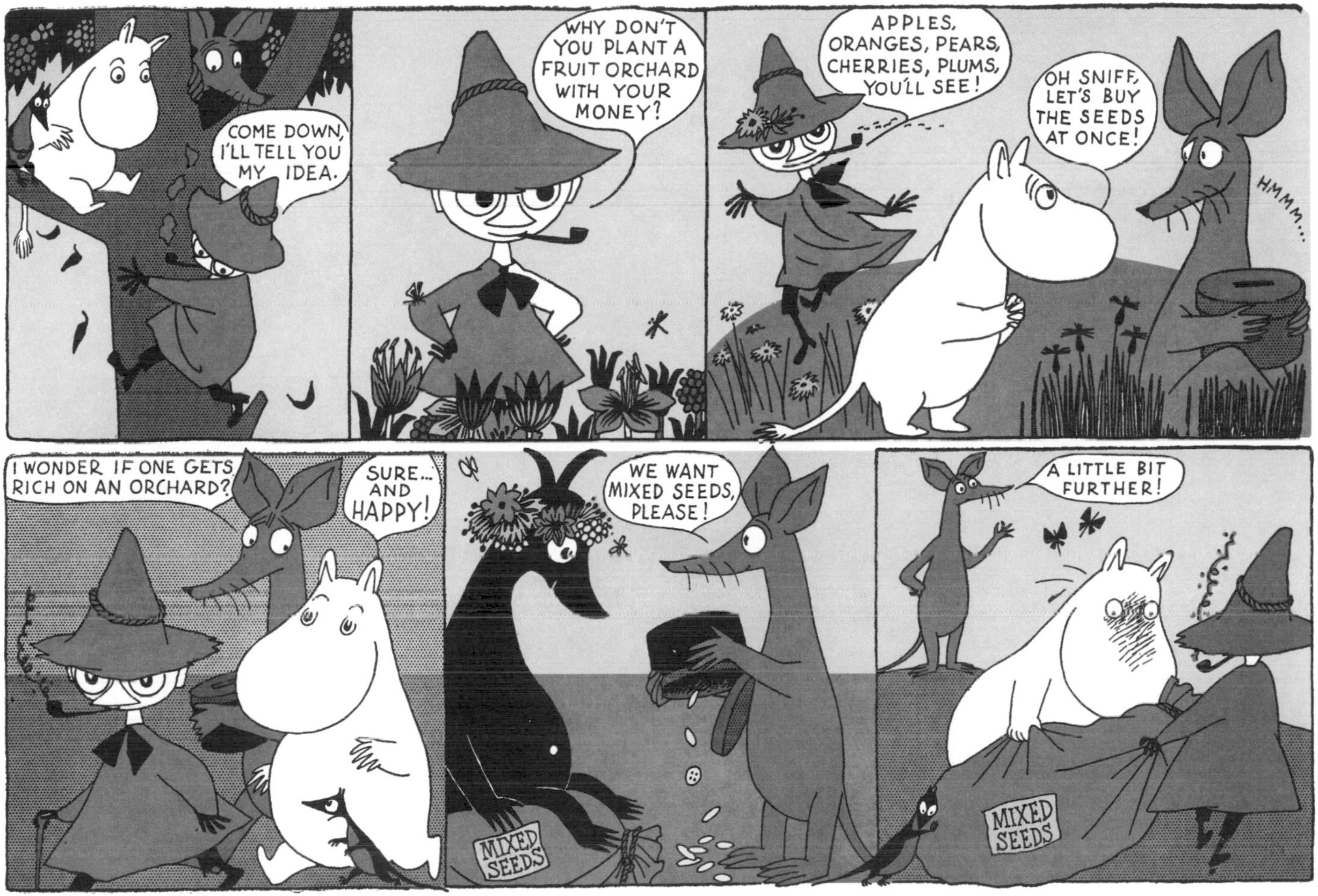
COME DOWN, I'LL TELL YOU MY IDEA.
WHY DON'T YOU PLANT A FRUIT ORCHARD WITH YOUR MONEY?
APPLES, ORANGES, PEARS, CHERRIES, PLUMS, YOU'LL SEE!
OH SNIFF, LET'S BUY THE SEEDS AT ONCE!
HMMM...
I WONDER IF ONE GETS RICH ON AN ORCHARD?
SURE... AND HAPPY!
WE WANT MIXED SEEDS, PLEASE!
MIXED SEEDS
A LITTLE BIT FURTHER!
MIXED SEEDS

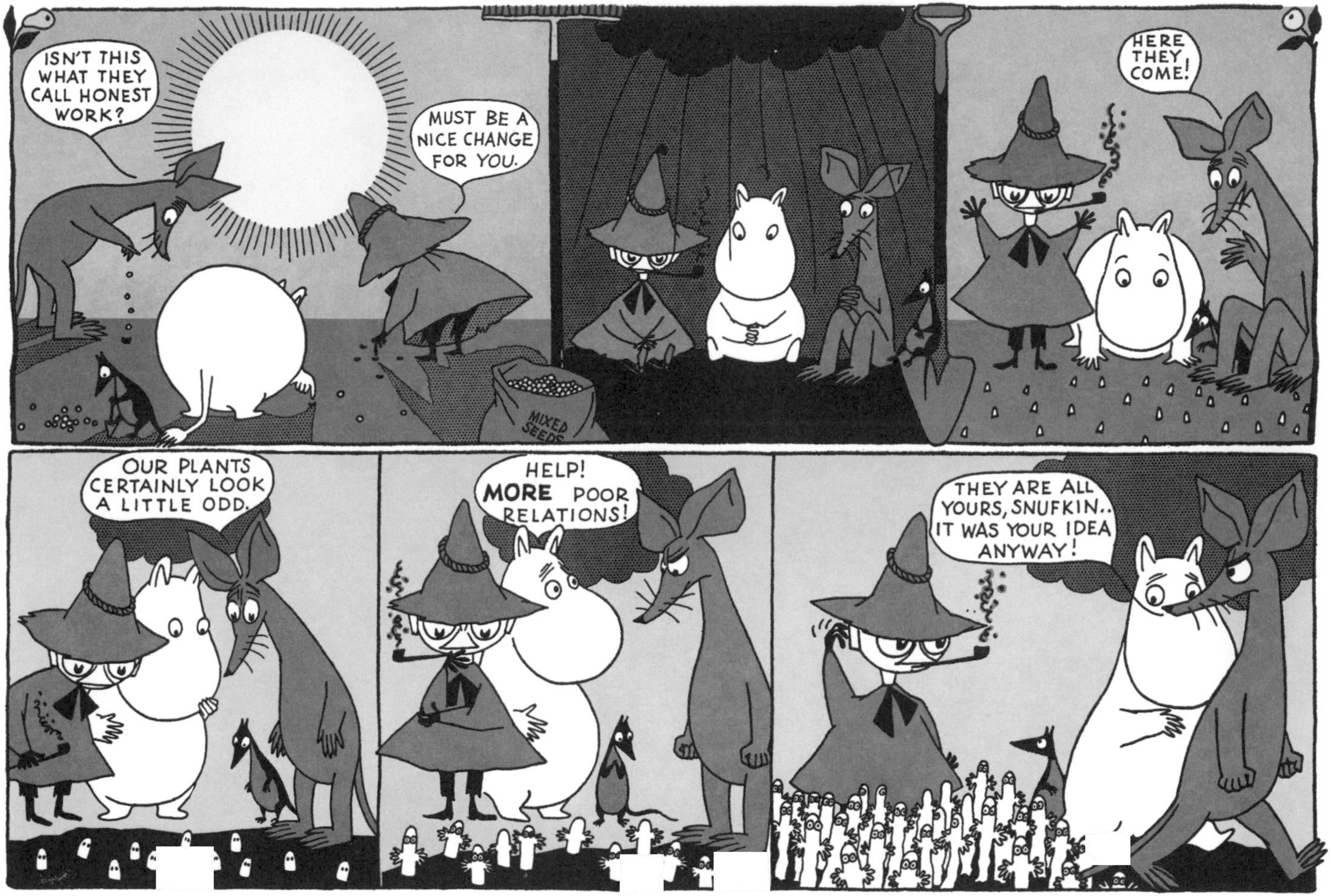
ISN'T THIS WHAT THEY CALL HONEST WORK?
MUST BE A NICE CHANGE FOR YOU.
MIXED SEEDS
HERE THEY COME!
OUR PLANTS CERTAINLY LOOK A LITTLE ODD.
HELP! MORE POOR RELATIONS!
THEY ARE ALL YOURS, SNUFKIN.. IT WAS YOUR IDEA ANYWAY!

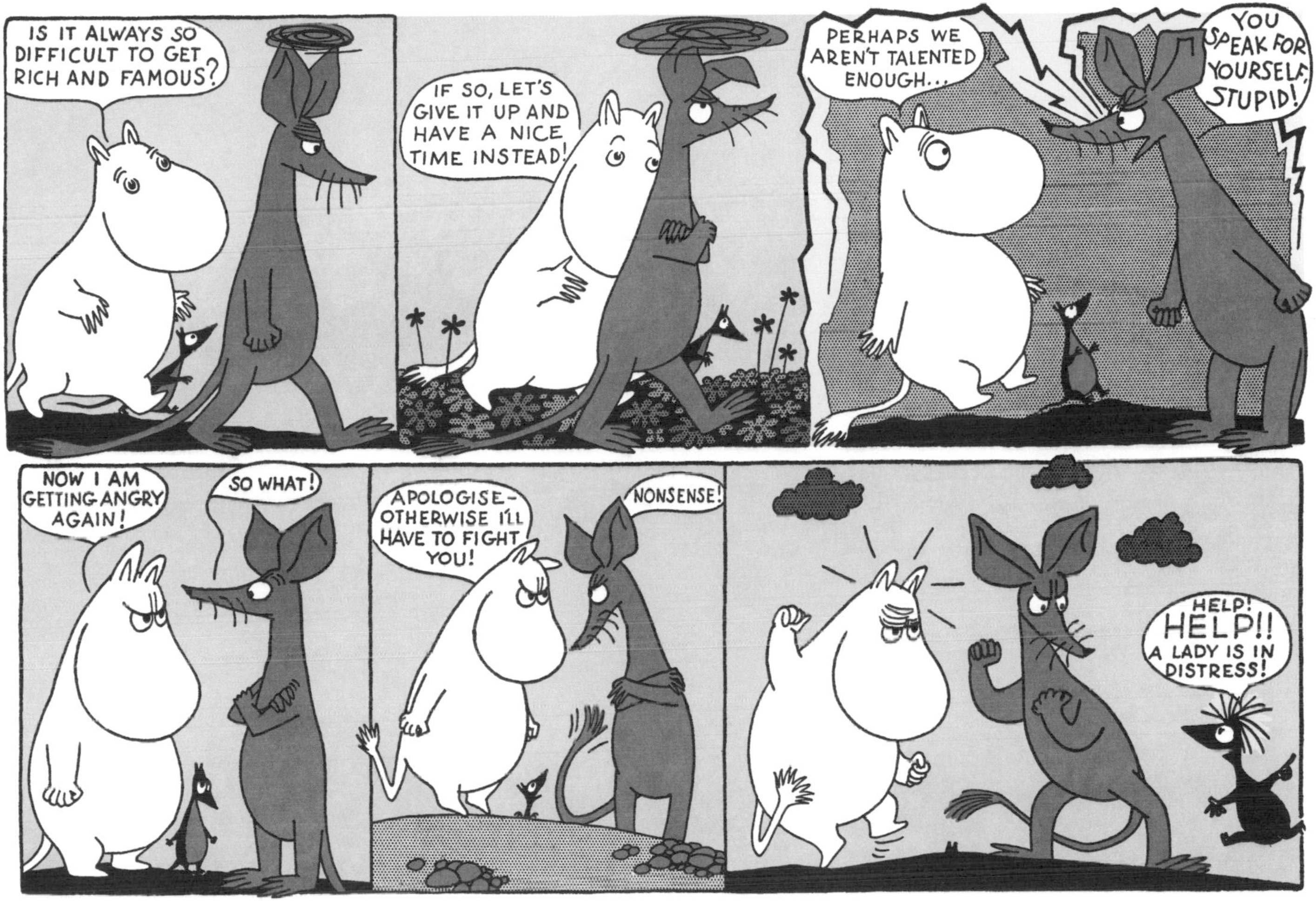
IS IT ALWAYS SO DIFFICULT TO GET RICH AND FAMOUS?
IF SO, LET'S GIVE IT UP AND HAVE A NICE TIME INSTEAD!
PERHAPS WE AREN'T TALENTED ENOUGH...
YOU SPEAK FOR YOURSELF, STUPID!
NOW I AM GETTING ANGRY AGAIN!
SO WHAT!
APOLOGISE- OTHERWISE I'LL HAVE TO FIGHT YOU!
NONSENSE!
HELP! HELP!! A LADY IS IN DISTRESS!

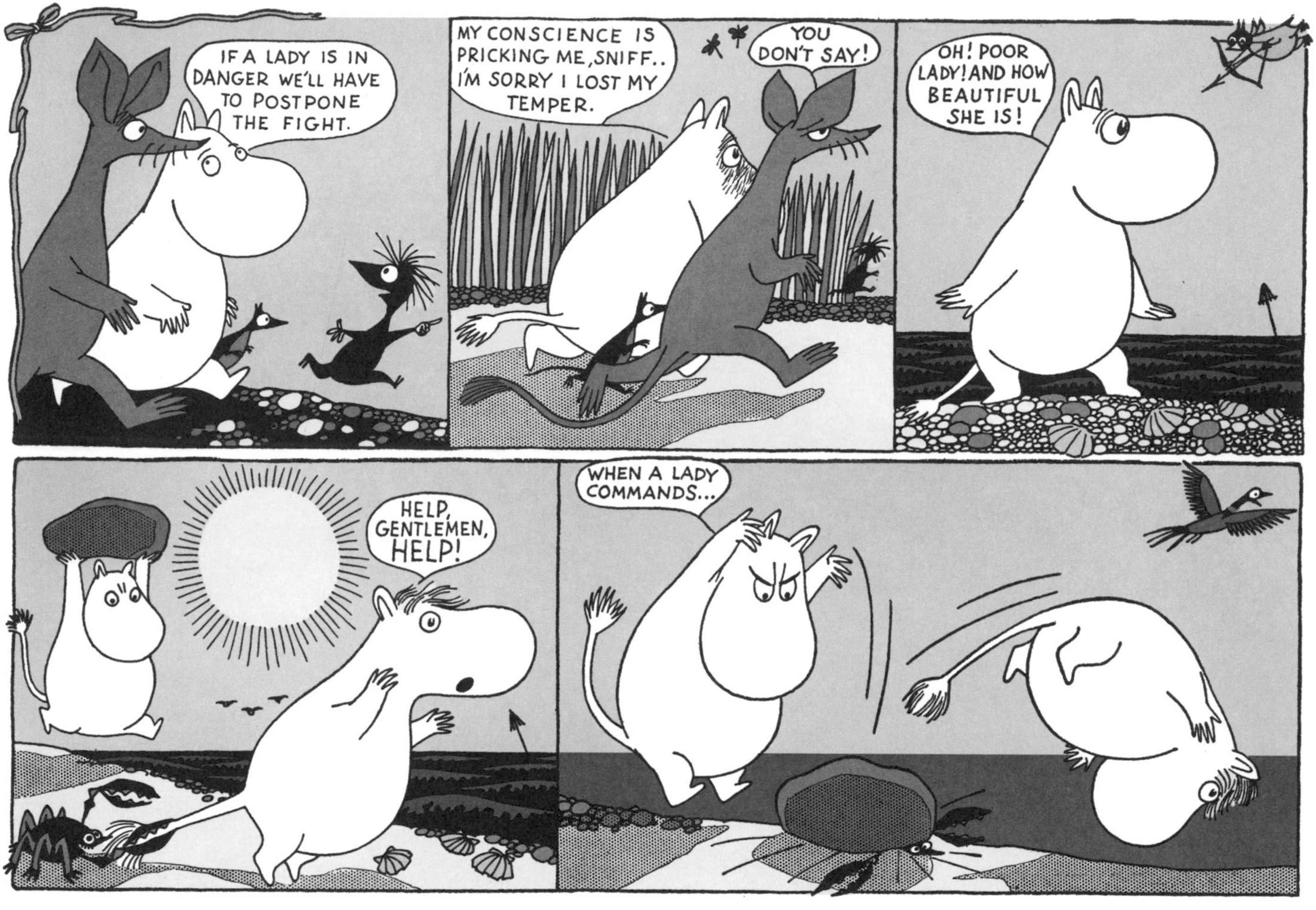
IF A LADY IS IN DANGER WE'LL HAVE TO POSTPONE THE FIGHT.
MY CONSCIENCE IS PRICKING ME, SNIFF.. I'M SORRY I LOST MY TEMPER.
YOU DON'T SAY!
OH! POOR LADY! AND HOW BEAUTIFUL SHE IS!
HELP, GENTLEMEN, HELP!
WHEN A LADY COMMANDS...

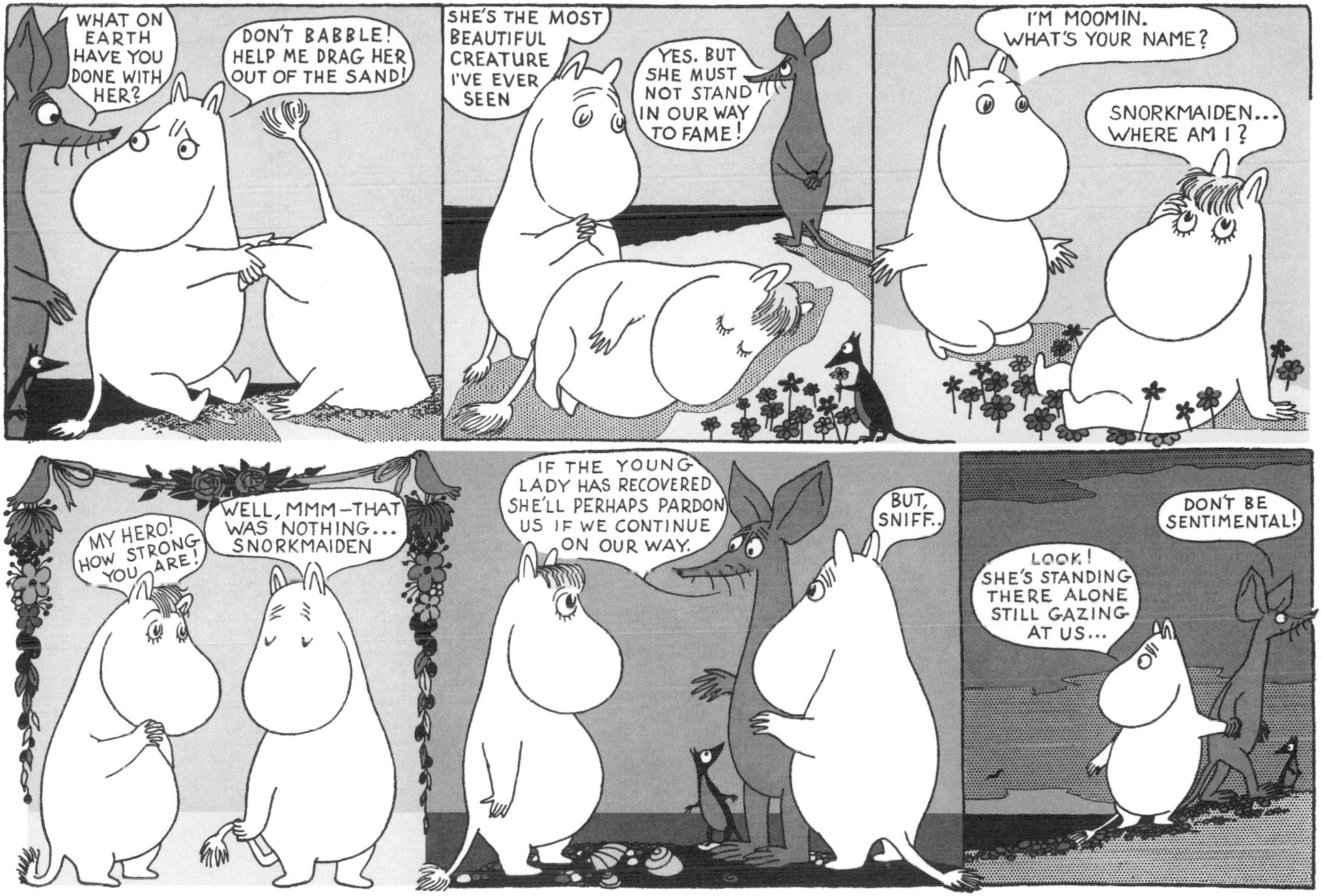
WHAT ON EARTH HAVE YOU DONE WITH HER?
DON'T BABBLE! HELP ME DRAG HER OUT OF THE SAND!
SHE'S THE MOST BEAUTIFUL CREATURE I'VE EVER SEEN
YES. BUT SHE MUST NOT STAND IN OUR WAY TO FAME!
I'M MOOMIN. WHAT'S YOUR NAME?
SNORKMAIDEN... WHERE AM I?
MY HERO! HOW STRONG YOU ARE!
WELL, MMM—THAT WAS NOTHING... SNORKMAIDEN
IF THE YOUNG LADY HAS RECOVERED SHE'LL PERHAPS PARDON US IF WE CONTINUE ON OUR WAY.
BUT, SNIFF..
DON'T BE SENTIMENTAL!
LOOK! SHE'S STANDING THERE ALONE STILL GAZING AT US...

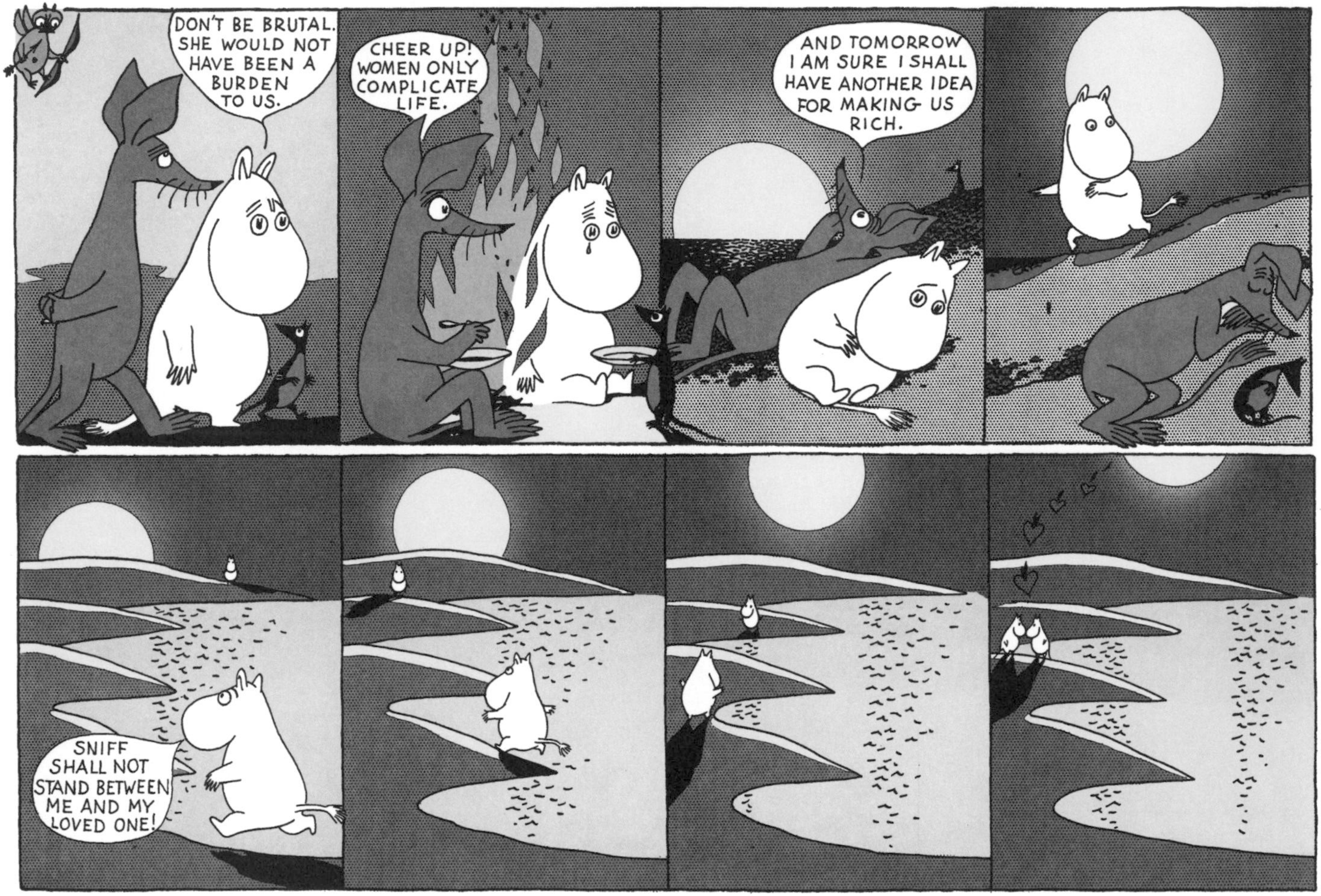
DON'T BE BRUTAL. SHE WOULD NOT HAVE BEEN A BURDEN TO US.
CHEER UP! WOMEN ONLY COMPLICATE LIFE.
AND TOMORROW I AM SURE I SHALL HAVE ANOTHER IDEA FOR MAKING US RICH.
SNIFF SHALL NOT STAND BETWEEN ME AND MY LOVED ONE!

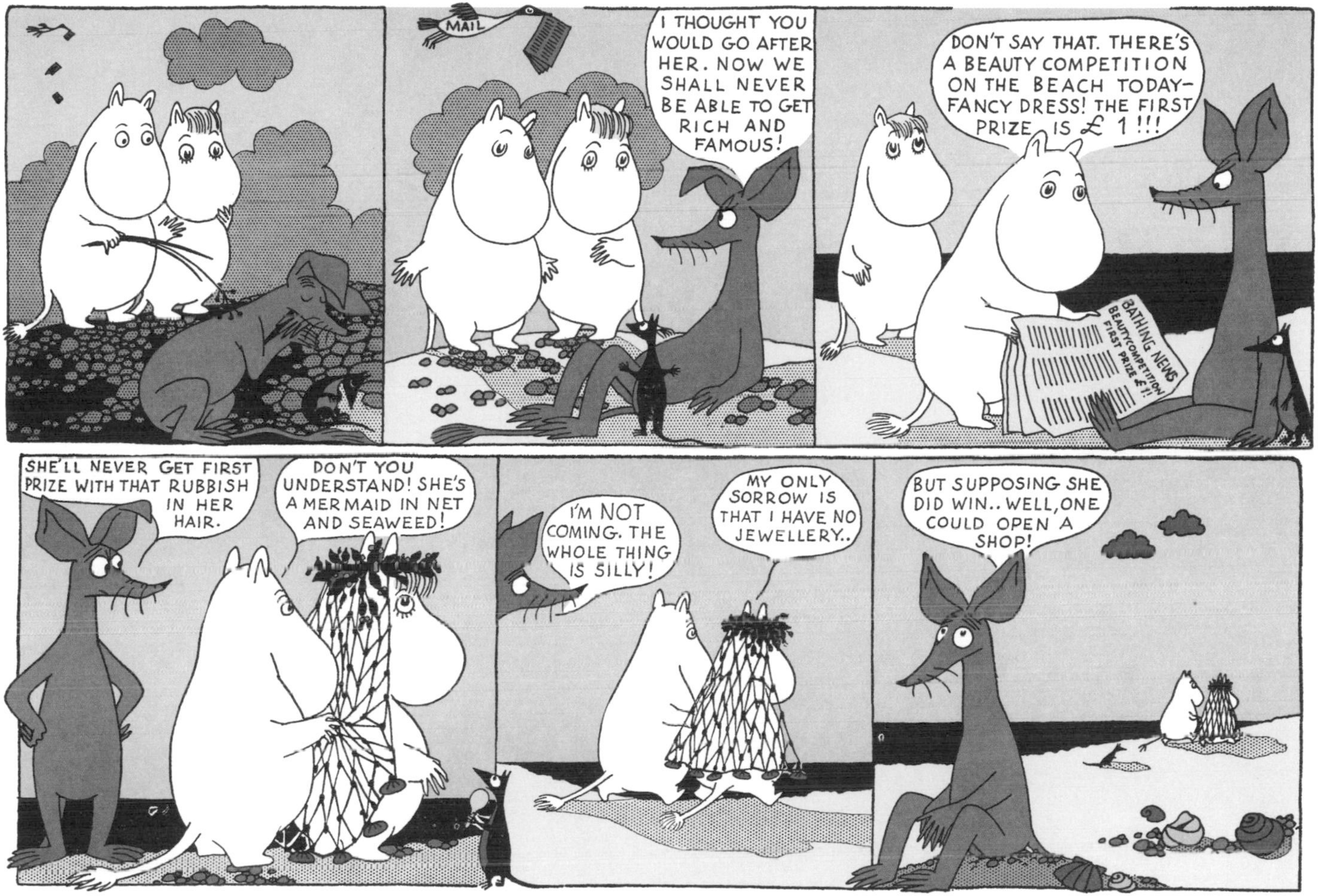
MAIL
I THOUGHT YOU WOULD GO AFTER HER. NOW WE SHALL NEVER BE ABLE TO GET RICH AND FAMOUS!
DON'T SAY THAT. THERE'S A BEAUTY COMPETITION ON THE BEACH TODAY- FANCY DRESS! THE FIRST PRIZE IS £ 1 !!!
BATHING NEWS
BEAUTYCOMPETITION
FIRST PRIZE £ 1!
SHE'LL NEVER GET FIRST PRIZE WITH THAT RUBBISH IN HER HAIR.
DON'T YOU UNDERSTAND! SHE'S A MERMAID IN NET AND SEAWEED!
I'M NOT COMING. THE WHOLE THING IS SILLY!
MY ONLY SORROW IS THAT I HAVE NO JEWELLERY..
BUT SUPPOSING SHE DID WIN.. WELL, ONE COULD OPEN A SHOP!

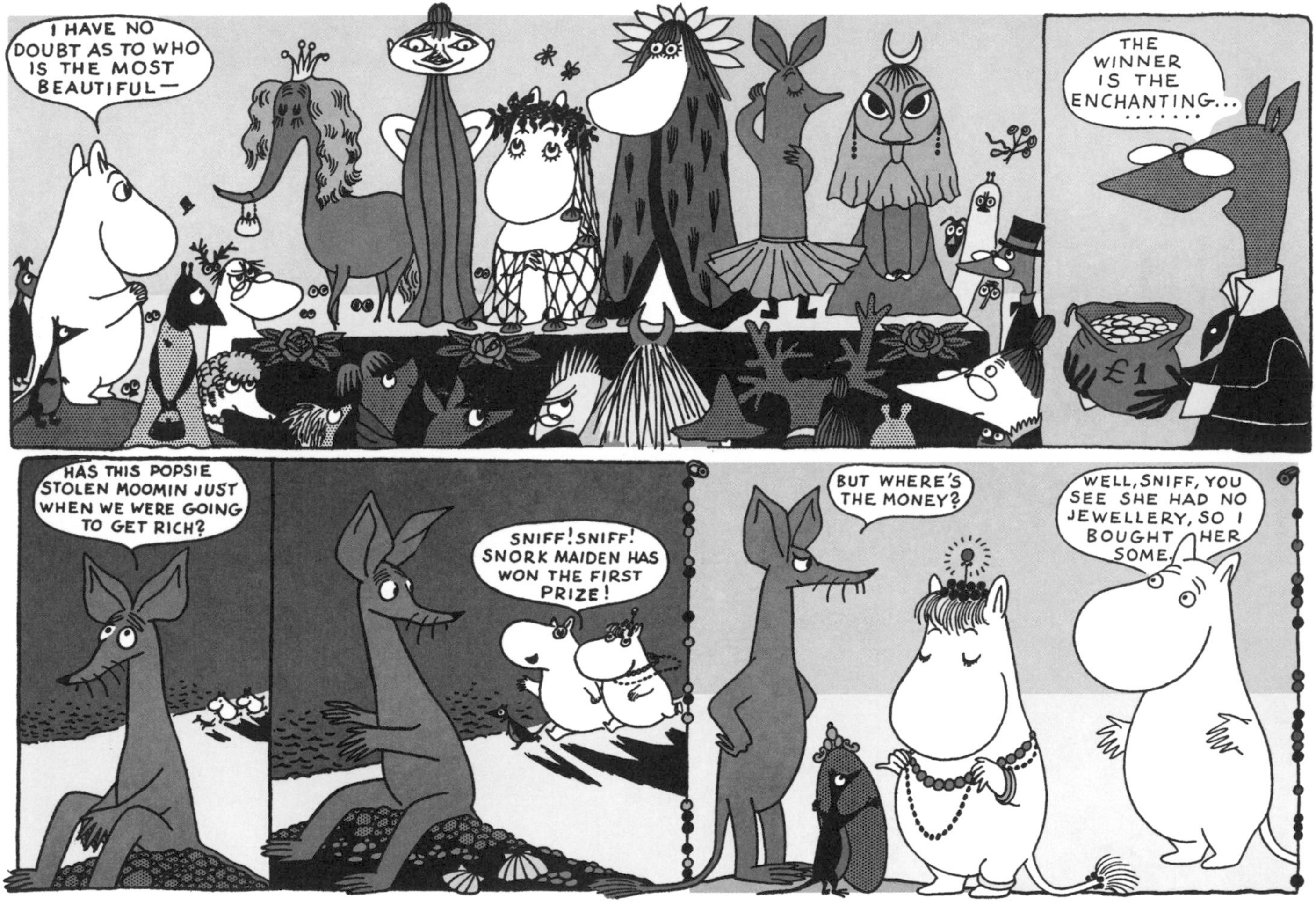
I HAVE NO DOUBT AS TO WHO IS THE MOST BEAUTIFUL—
THE WINNER IS THE ENCHANTING........
£1
HAS THIS POPSIE STOLEN MOOMIN JUST WHEN WE WERE GOING TO GET RICH?
SNIFF! SNIFF! SNORK MAIDEN HAS WON THE FIRST PRIZE!
BUT WHERE'S THE MONEY?
WELL, SNIFF, YOU SEE SHE HAD NO JEWELLERY, SO I BOUGHT HER SOME.

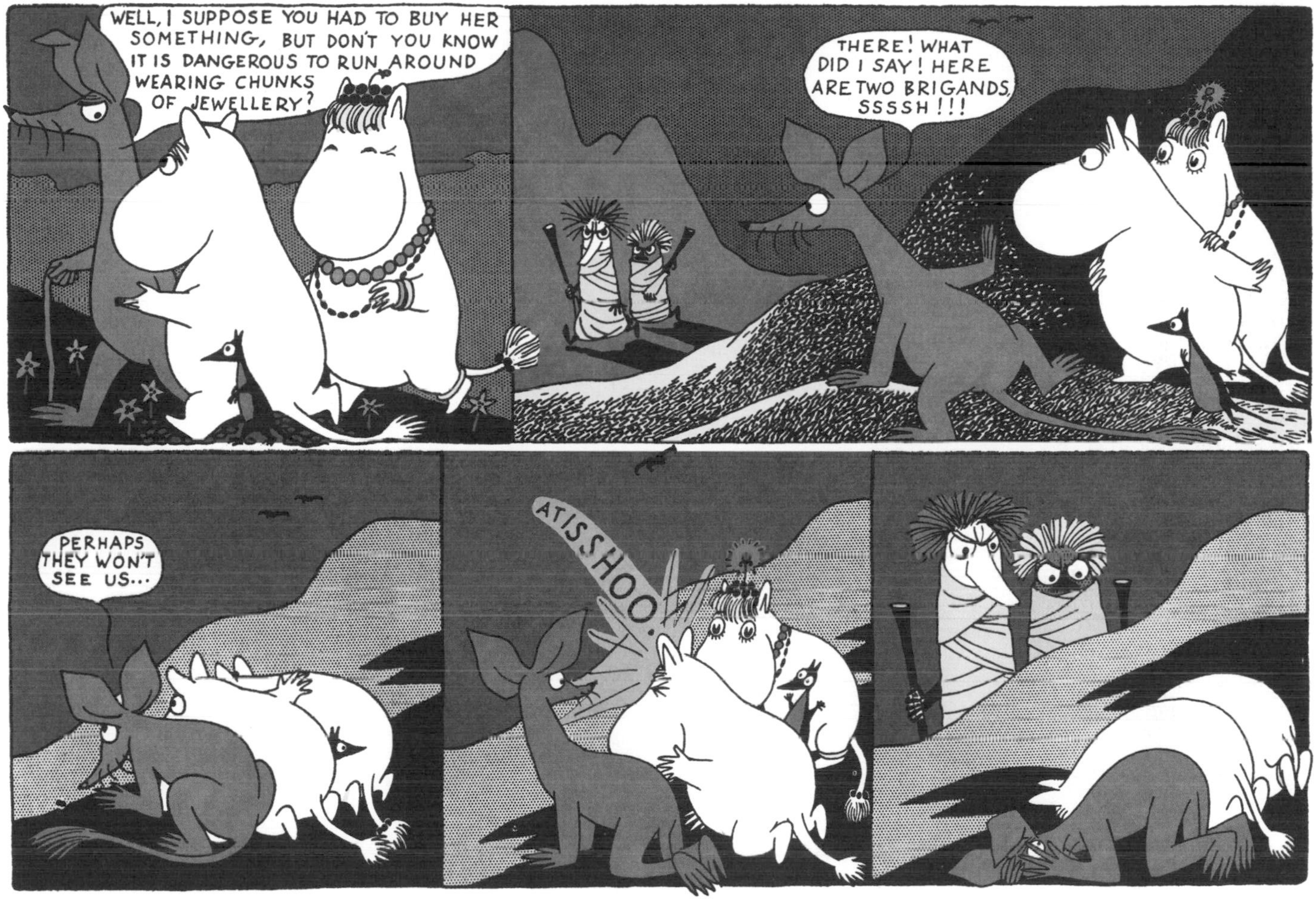
WELL, I SUPPOSE YOU HAD TO BUY HER SOMETHING, BUT DON'T YOU KNOW IT IS DANGEROUS TO RUN AROUND WEARING CHUNKS OF JEWELLERY?
THERE! WHAT DID I SAY! HERE ARE TWO BRIGANDS. SSSSH!!!
PERHAPS THEY WON'T SEE US...
ATISSHOO!

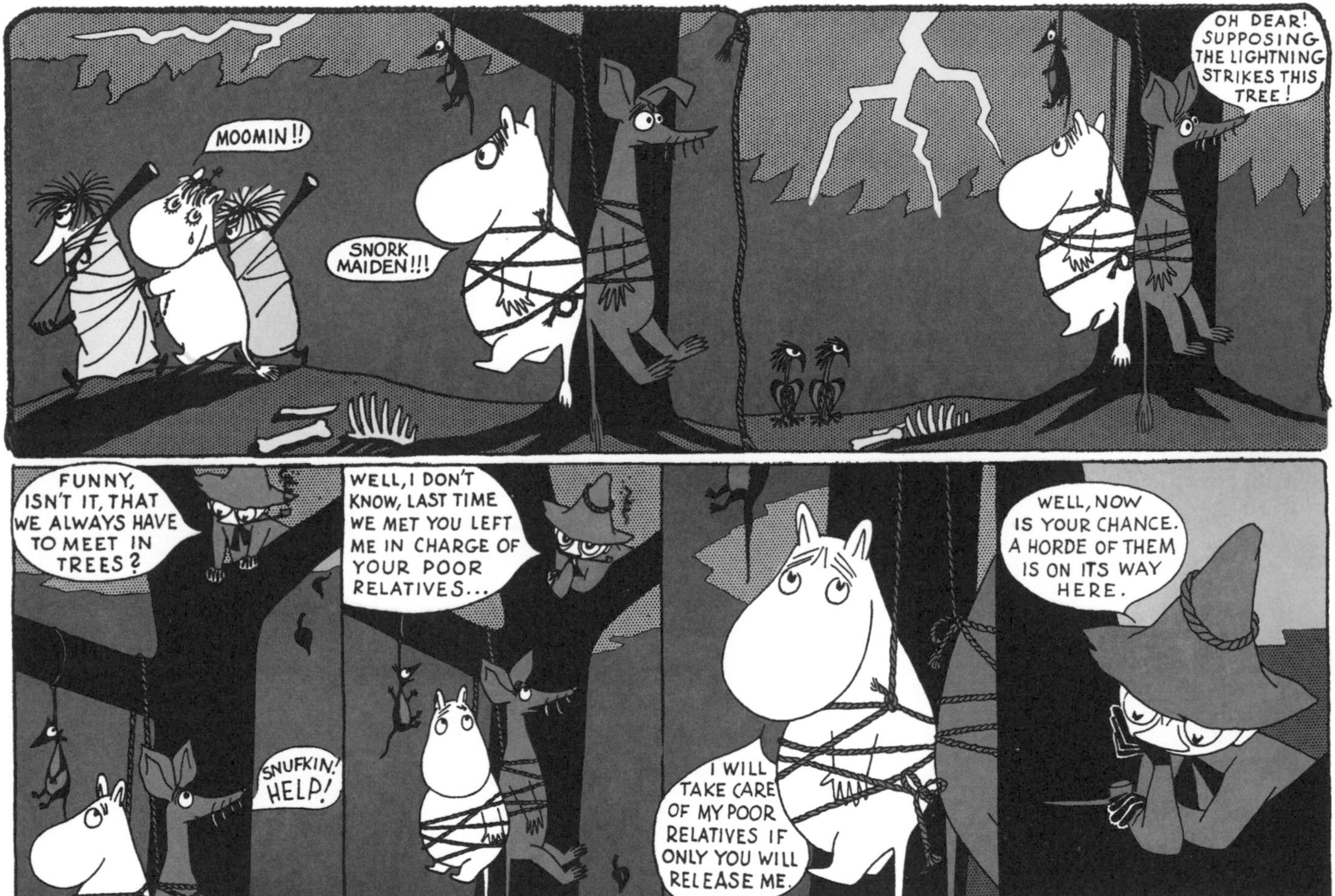
MOOMIN!!
SNORK MAIDEN!!!
OH DEAR! SUPPOSING THE LIGHTNING STRIKES THIS TREE!
SNUFKIN! HELP!
FUNNY, ISN'T IT, THAT WE ALWAYS HAVE TO MEET IN TREES?
WELL, I DON'T KNOW, LAST TIME WE MET YOU LEFT ME IN CHARGE OF YOUR POOR RELATIVES...
I WILL TAKE CARE OF MY POOR RELATIVES IF ONLY YOU WILL RELEASE ME.
WELL, NOW IS YOUR CHANCE. A HORDE OF THEM IS ON ITS WAY HERE.

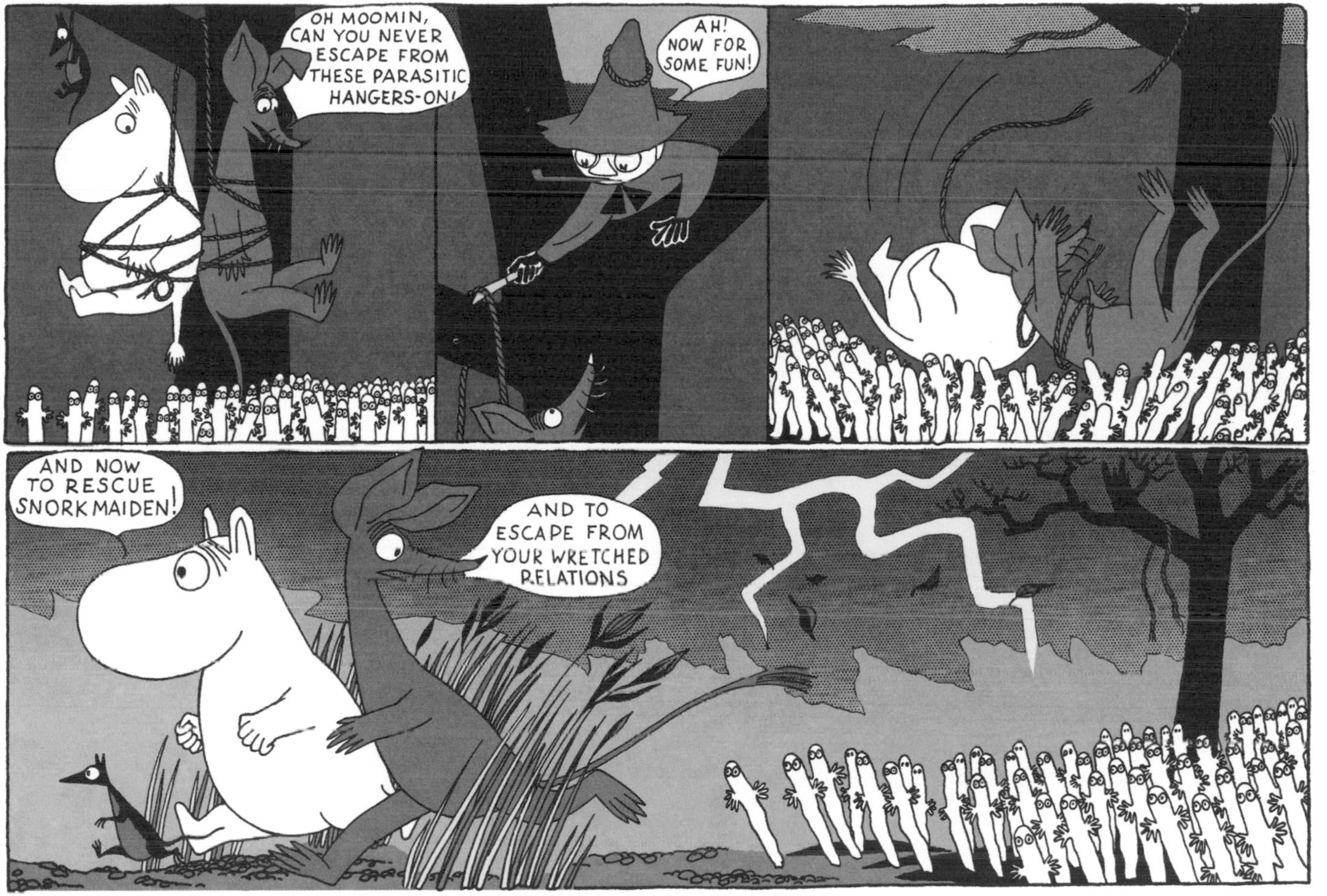
OH MOOMIN, CAN YOU NEVER ESCAPE FROM THESE PARASITIC HANGERS-ON!
AH! NOW FOR SOME FUN!
AND NOW TO RESCUE SNORKMAIDEN!
AND TO ESCAPE FROM YOUR WRETCHED RELATIONS

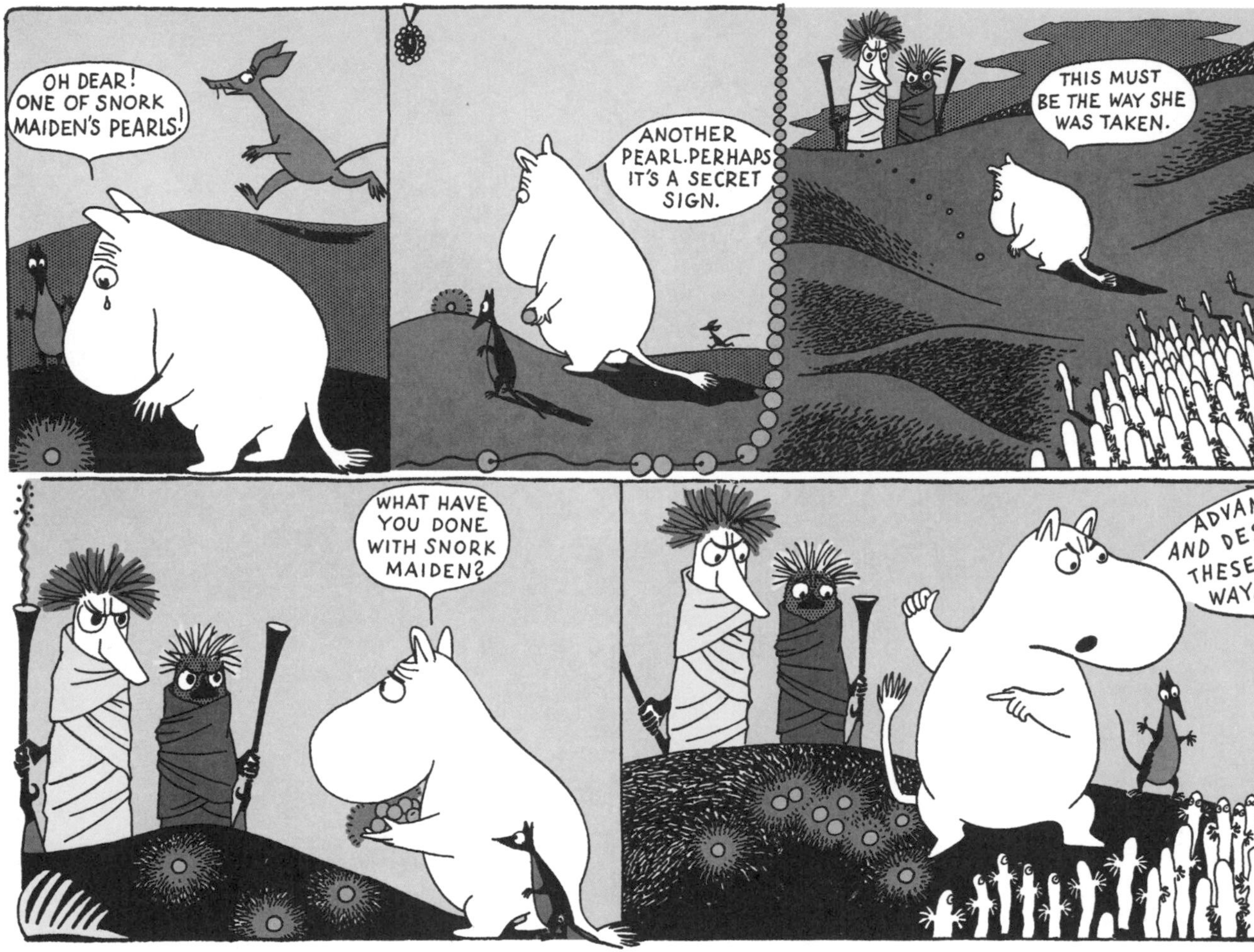
OH DEAR! ONE OF SNORK MAIDEN'S PEARLS!
ANOTHER PEARL. PERHAPS IT'S A SECRET SIGN.
THIS MUST BE THE WAY SHE WAS TAKEN.
WHAT HAVE YOU DONE WITH SNORK MAIDEN?
ADVANCE AND DESTROY THESE HIGH-WAYMEN!

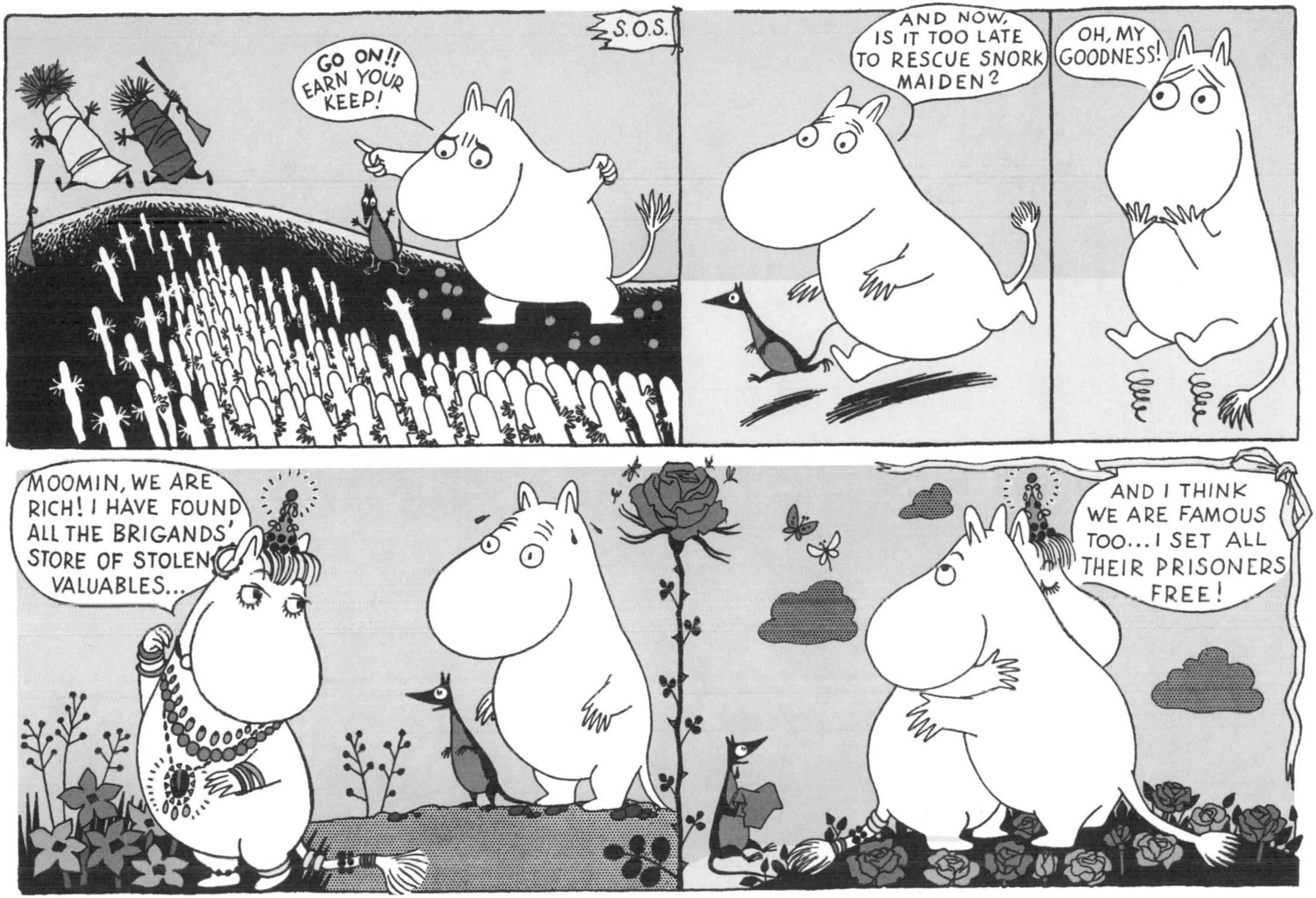

S.O.S.
GO ON!! EARN YOUR KEEP!
AND NOW, IS IT TOO LATE TO RESCUE SNORK MAIDEN?
OH, MY GOODNESS!
MOOMIN, WE ARE RICH! I HAVE FOUND ALL THE BRIGANDS' STORE OF STOLEN VALUABLES...
AND I THINK WE ARE FAMOUS TOO... I SET ALL THEIR PRISONERS FREE!

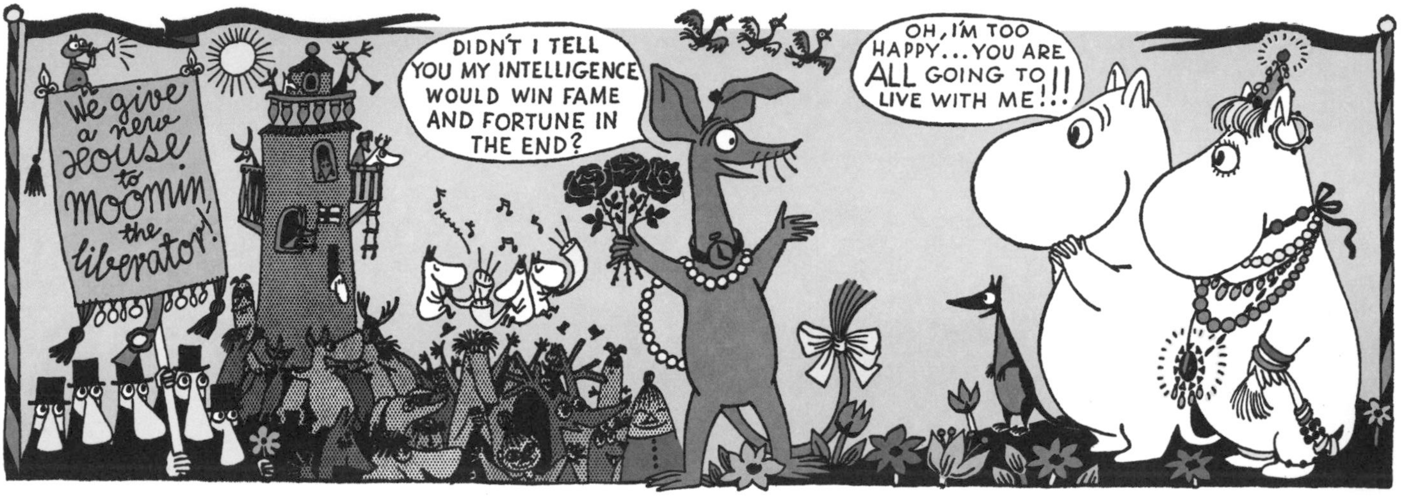
We give a new House to Moomin, the liberator!
DIDN'T I TELL YOU MY INTELLIGENCE WOULD WIN FAME AND FORTUNE IN THE END?
OH, I'M TOO HAPPY... YOU ARE ALL GOING TO LIVE WITH ME!!!

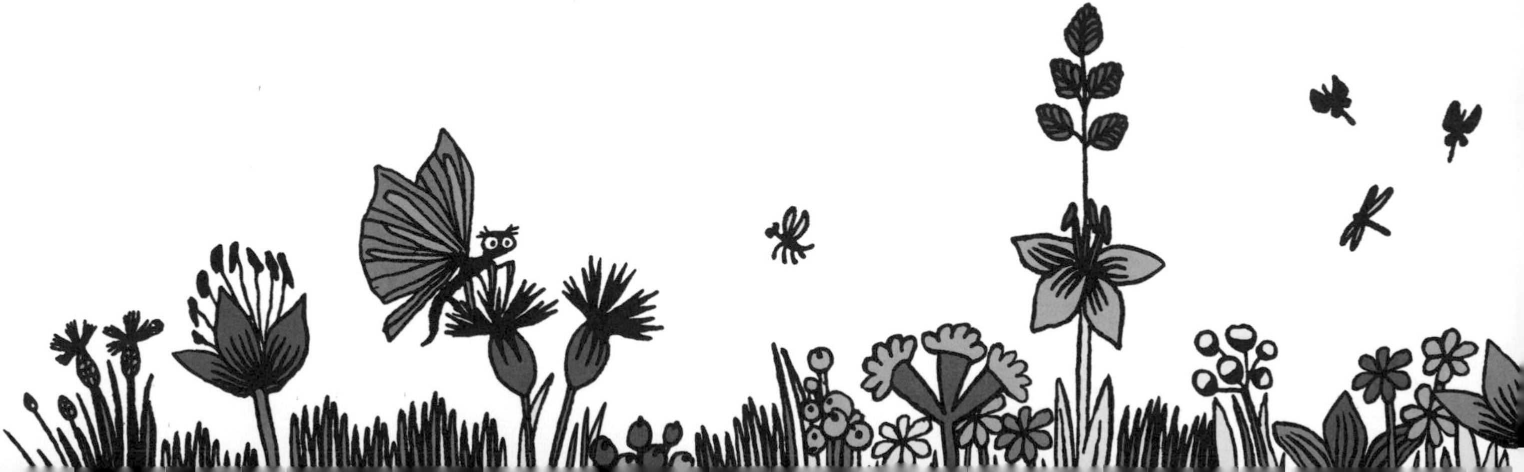

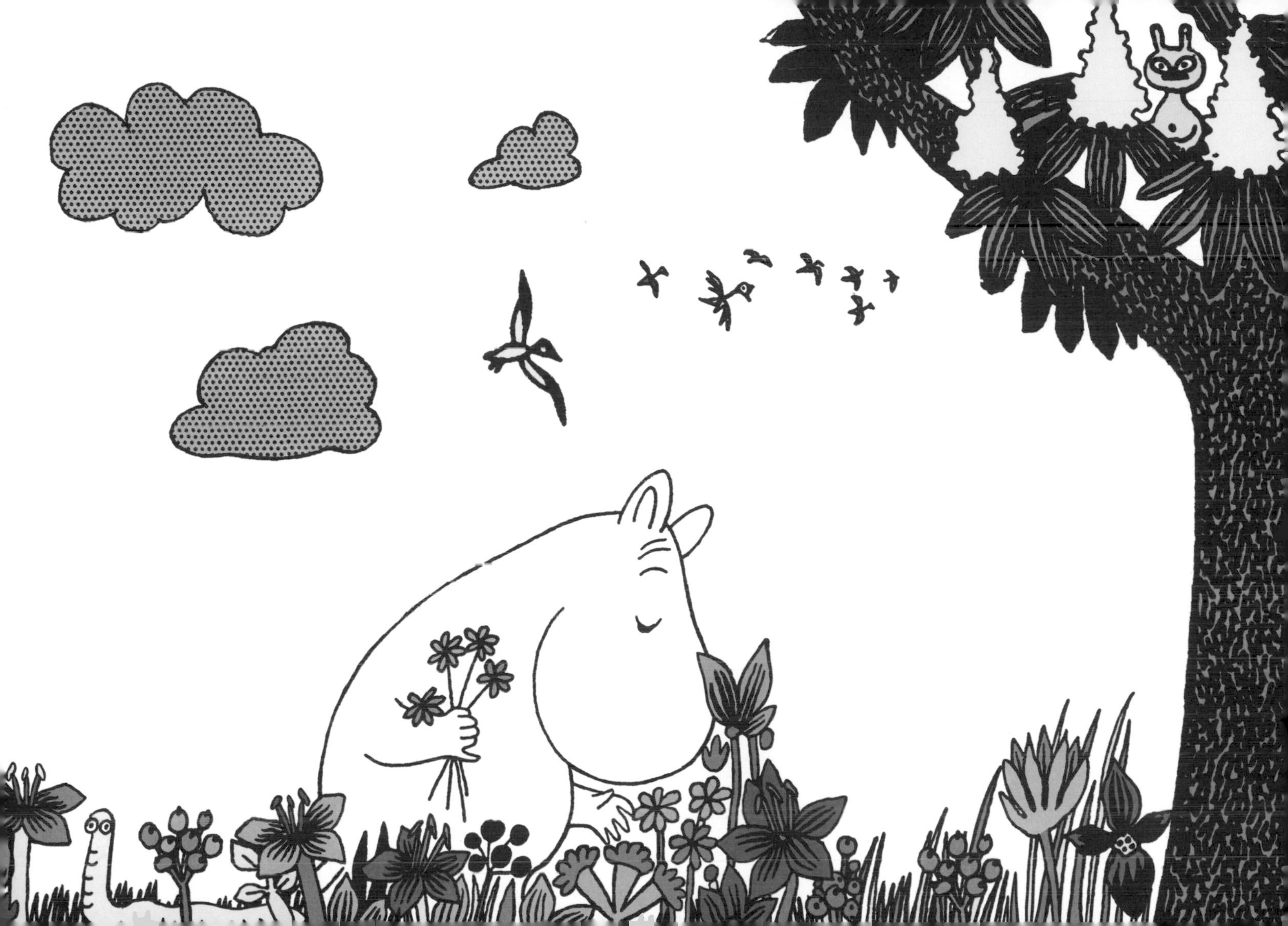

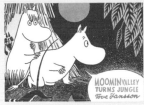

MOOMINVALLEY TURNS JUNGLE
Tove Jansson
Moominvalley Turns Jungle

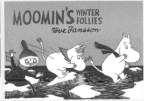

MOOMIN'S WINTER FOLLIES
Tove Jansson
Moomin's Winter Follies

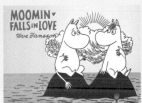

MOOMIN FALLS IN LOVE
Tove Jansson
Moomin Falls in Love

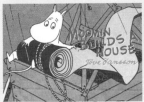

MOOMIN BUILDS A HOUSE
Tove Jansson
Moomin Builds a House

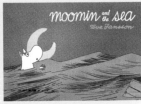

moomin and the sea
Tove Jansson
Moomin and the Sea

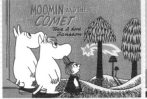

MOOMIN AND THE COMET
Tove & Lars Jansson
Moomin and the Comet

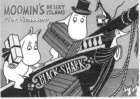

MOOMIN'S DESERT ISLAND
Tove Jansson
FIREWORKS
BLACK SHARK
Moomin's Desert Island

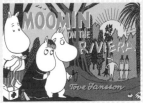

MOOMIN ON THE RIVIERA
Tove Jansson
Moomin on the Riviera

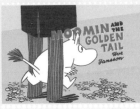

MOOMIN AND THE GOLDEN TAIL
Tove Jansson
Moomin and the Golden Tail

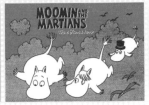

MOOMIN AND THE MARTIANS
Tove Jansson
Moomin and the Martians

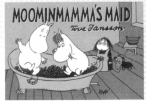

MOOMINMAMMA'S MAID
Tove Jansson
Moominmamma's Maid

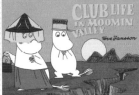

CLUB LIFE IN MOOMIN VALLEY
Tove Jansson
Club Life in Moominvalley

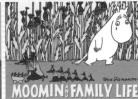

Tove Jansson
MOOMIN AND FAMILY LIFE
Moomin and Family Life

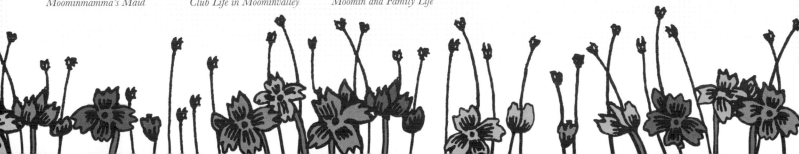

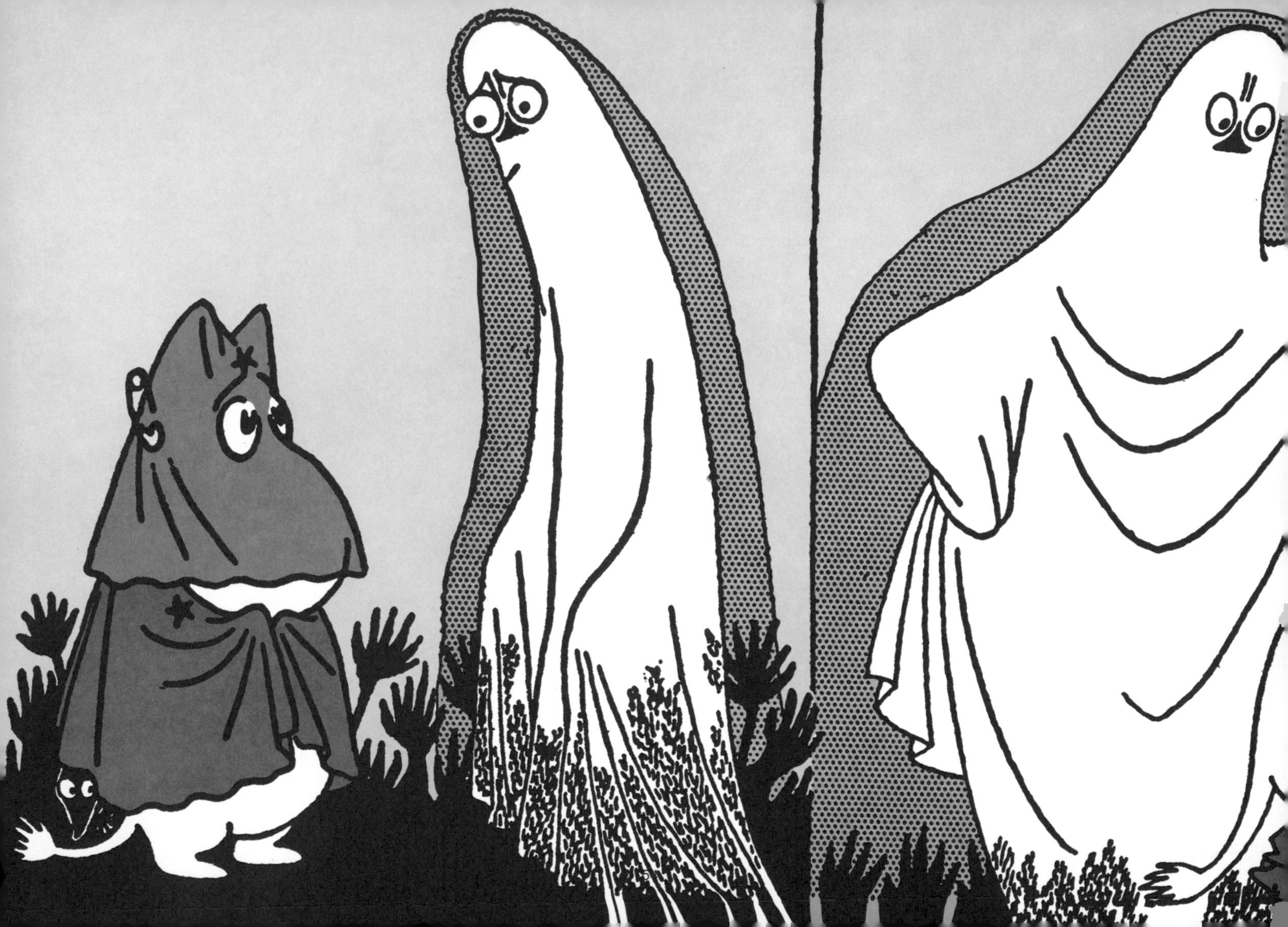

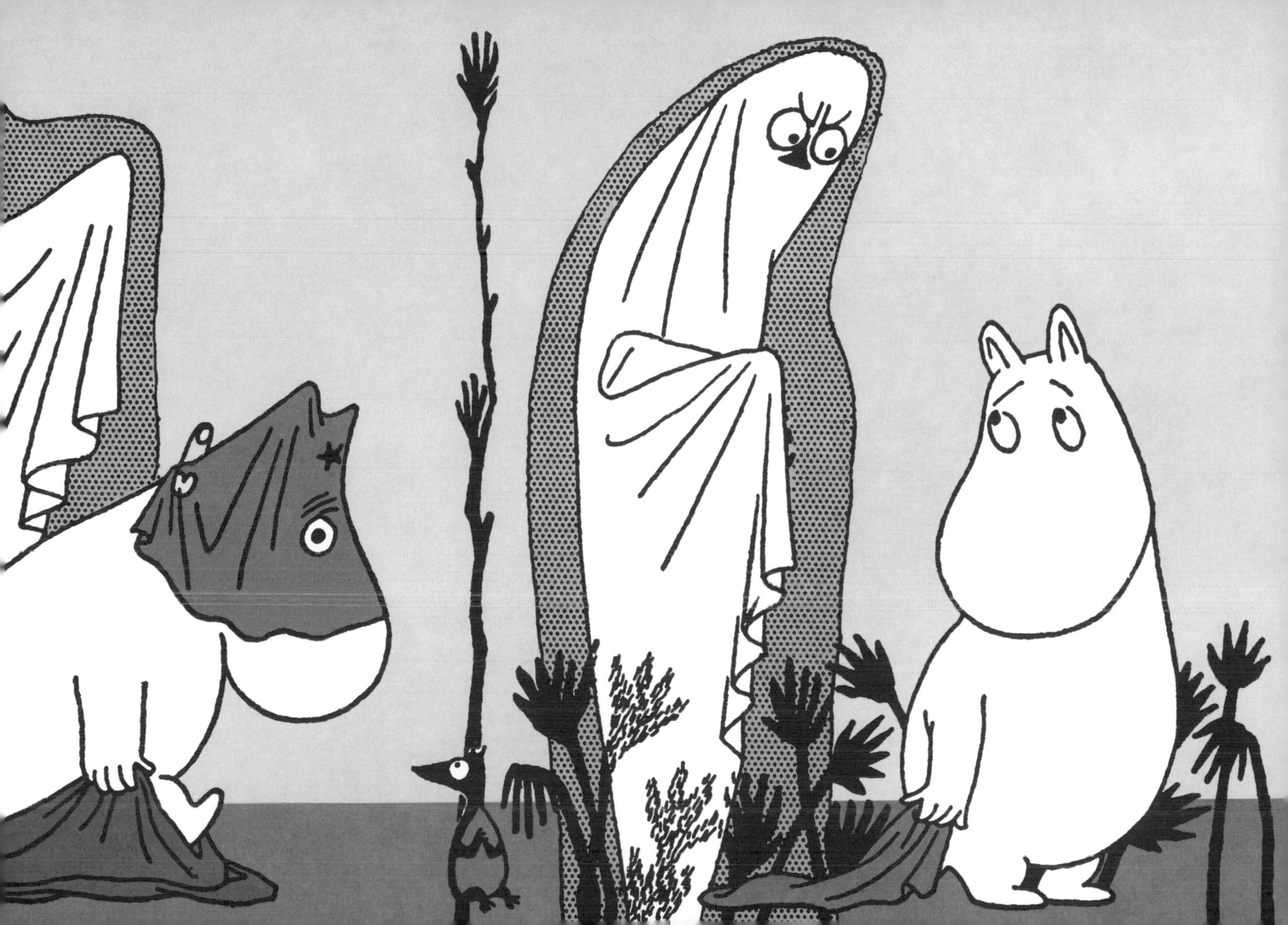

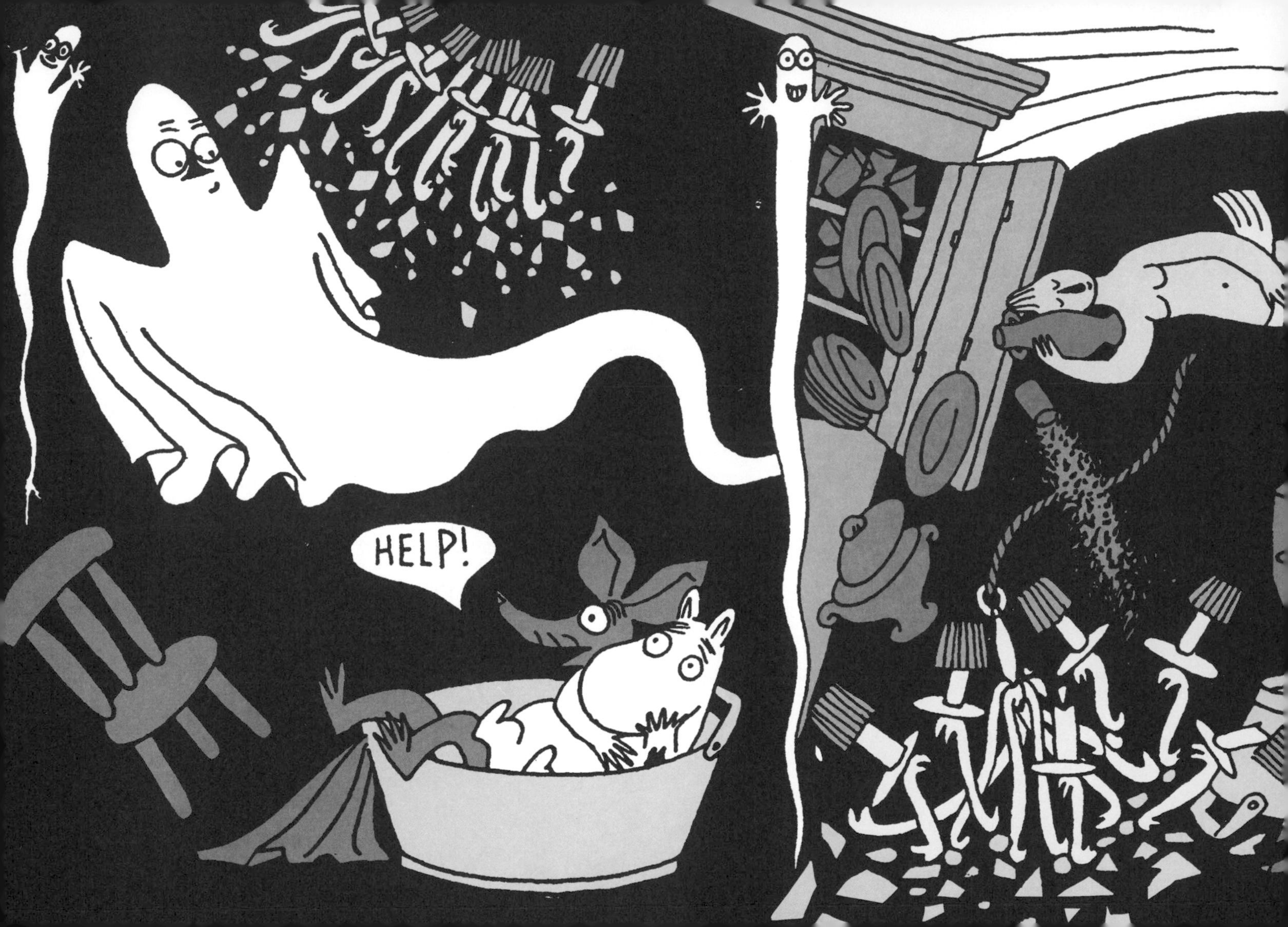
HELP!

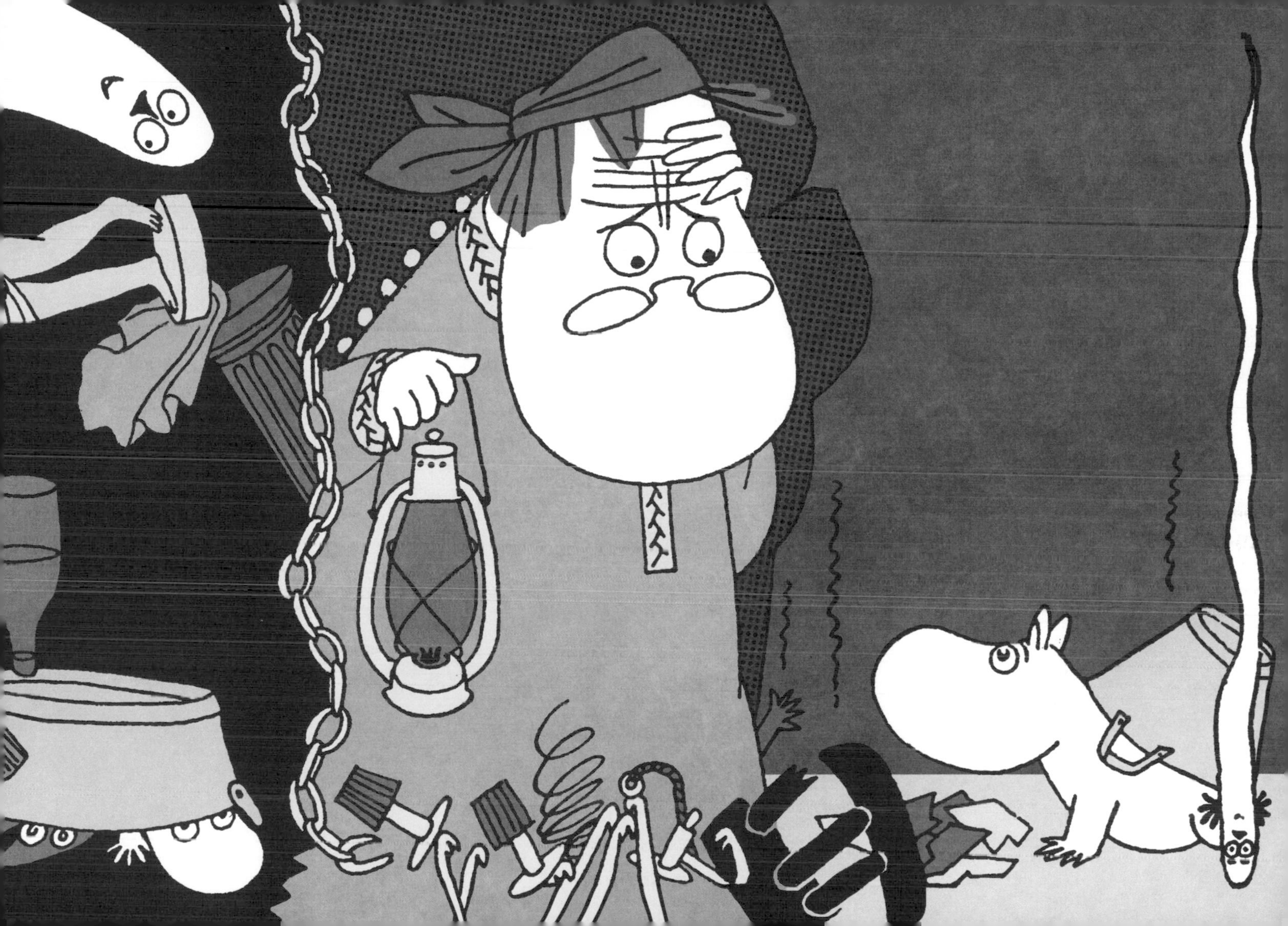

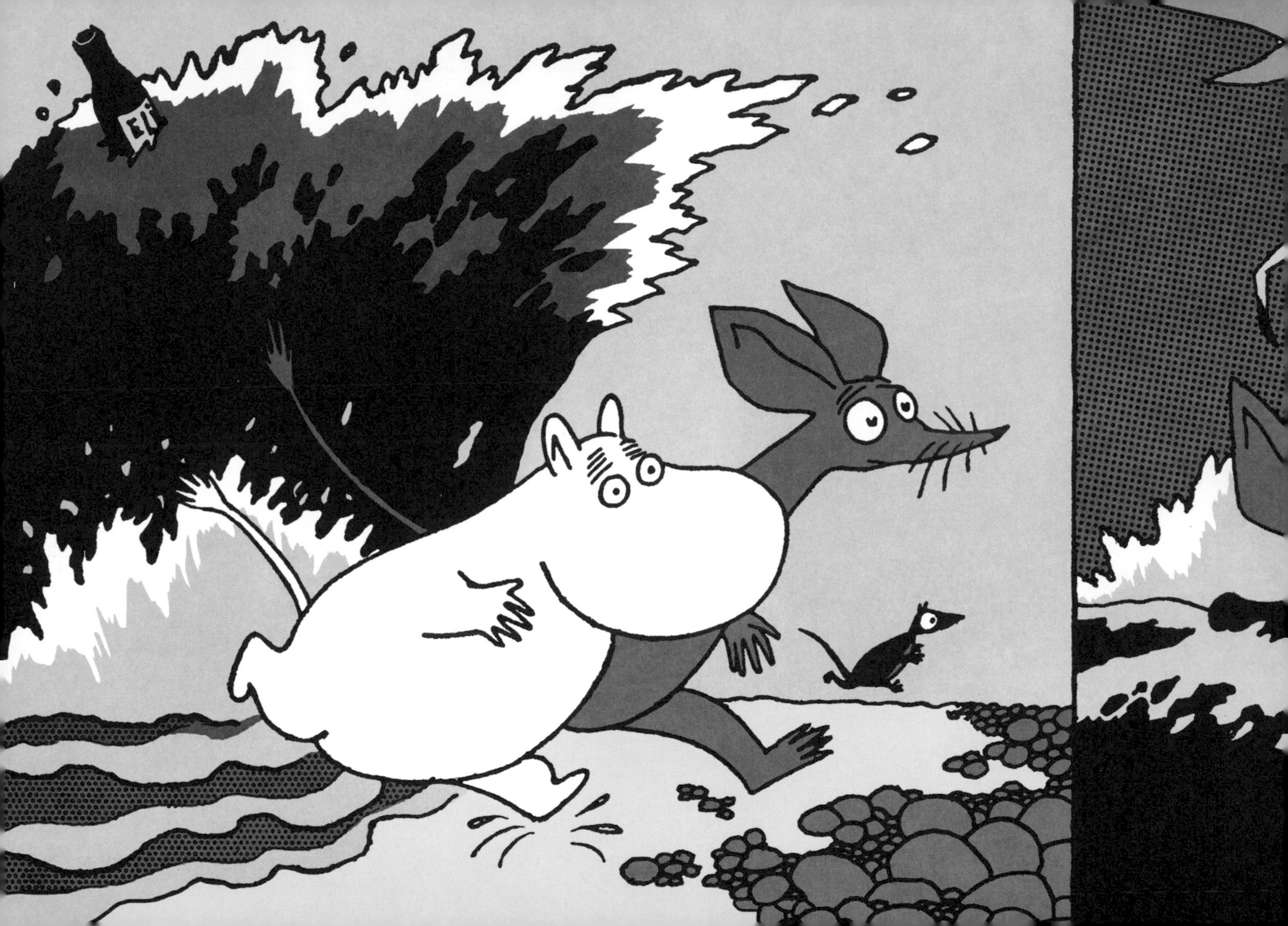